GRINGO

Walt Parras wakes up at the bottom of a cliff beside his horse . . . which has a bullet-hole in its head. When he stumbles out of the brush — stubbled, scarred and bloodstained — and fetches up at the Two-Pole Pumpkin ranch, the owner's daughter Teresa Romero takes pity on him and offers him work. Though keen to earn his keep, Parras remembers nothing at all from the time before he regained consciousness, and only knows his own name because it appears on the papers he carries . . . Trouble has been building on the ranch for some time. As the elderly Don Adolfo Romero crawls further into a bottle every day, despite his daughter's efforts to stop him and keep the ranch running, the ramrod Olivares seems to be quietly taking over control of the spread. Meanwhile, Parras begins to fall in love with Teresa . . .

GRINGO

NELSON NYE

SAGEBRUSH
Large Print Westerns

First published in Great Britain by ISIS Publishing Ltd.
First published in the United States by Ace Books

First Isis Edition
published 2017
by arrangement with
Golden West Literary Agency

A catalogue record for this book is available
from the British Library.

ISBN 978–1–78541–399–5 (pb)

Published by
F. A. Thorpe (Publishing)
Anstey, Leicestershire

Set by Words & Graphics Ltd.
Anstey, Leicestershire
Printed and bound in Great Britain by
T. J. International Ltd., Padstow, Cornwall

This book is printed on acid-free paper

CHAPTER
ONE

"What place is this?"

"What place are you looking for?"

"I don't know," he said at the edge of the porch, and they stared at each other through an interval of silence while the girl considered his hard-used appearance and knew with a thoughtful narrowing of eyes that she was completely alone with this beard-stubbled stranger.

In the brush-clawed clothes and scuffed Justins, with those rope-scarred hands and sun-blackened cheeks, he had the look of a breed this range had seen more than enough of. The bloody rag tied Apache fashion around his head did nothing to detract from this overall impression and — with so much that was inimical pressing for decisions which outraged all she had been brought up to believe in — she unconsciously resented an assumption of equality coming from a man so obviously a gringo.

Still . . . he'd been hurt. This weighed with her, too.

Tightening her hold on the door she moistened dry lips. There were people she could call but no one near enough to hear; the huts of her father's peon help stood better than a quarter of a mile away, where their noise and smells could not intrude on family. The kitchen was at the other end of the house.

Peering at his heat-reddened eyes she said: "What happened to your mount?" and saw the jaws bite down.

"Reckon I must have got a mite careless — man shouldn't ride strange country in the dark." He said moments later in a testy grumble, "I woke up this morning 'longside a dead horse. At the bottom of a cliff."

The graphic way this last dug into that youthful face was not lost on him, its sharpening lines or the way her tongue crept again across red lips.

"You — you've been stumbling around through the brush ever since?"

"Twiddlin' my thumbs in the middle of nowhere with a stove-up canteen and the day getting hot enough to fry eggs anyplace ain't exactly my best notion for a long and happy life."

She looked concerned. Coming away from the door she reached down and held out the olla of water slung by a strap from one of the vigas. "Just a little now," she cautioned. "Don't try to empty it all at one gulp . . . "

"I wasn't born yesterday," he growled, taking hold of it.

He sloshed some around in his mouth and spat, took a second tiny swig, inscrutably considering the giver before swallowing.

This girl was quality. All the signs of it were there and he could understand her hesitancy, knowing he must look a saddle tramp or worse — and foreign besides.

He saw this much at once despite the queerness in his head. He could appreciate from the layout this was not headquarters for any two-bit operation.

The huge square house was built in the fashion of a fortress with narrow grated slits cut into it for windows with the walls thick enough to stand off even cannon. The big double-doored gate that swung from massive hinges was of great hewn logs strapped together with broad bands of hand-hammered iron and probably led to some inner courtyard or patio used in wilder days to protect the outfit's horses, perhaps the families of its riders.

This porch had been tacked on much later, a concession maybe to the influx of Texicans that in the past several years had overrun this region like a plague of hungry locusts.

With a slanchways glance at the girl's distrustful eyes, he decided he was thankful to be here, able still to appreciate the firm full-fleshed lines of her provocative figure.

He took another drink, holding it again behind the grip of strong teeth before easing it along in carefully measured swallows. His scowl was for the hole he had found in the head of that dead horse.

"If it's work you're looking for," the girl said tentatively, "I suppose Olivares might turn up something for you. There's a bunkhouse over beyond the corrals where you may wait if you wish till he can spare the time to talk with you. Better take that jug with you."

If she'd hoped to dismiss him, his continuing presence, unspeaking, darkly staring, big hands still wrapped about the clay pot, must have proved unsettling.

Breathing faster she sneaked a glance toward the door, palpably regretting having stepped so far away from it.

And looked back at him, flustered. The odds against her reaching it in time appeared almighty long if it came into this fellow's head to prevent her. She considered the heavy gun strapped to his leg and, pulling up her chin, caught the tag end of a twisted smile.

But he stayed in his tracks, saying mildly enough, "I'd still like to know whereabouts I am."

"Two-Pole Pumpkin — the Romero outfit. Six miles off the road to Goose Flat. I," she said grandly, "am Teresa Romero."

He jerked a nod. "Walt Parras. That don't tell me a heap."

"What do you want to be told, Mr. Parras?"

"I don't know."

"Well . . . what place are you hunting?"

"Don't know that, either."

He watched her tongue cross the red lips again. "You don't have to roll them eyes at me, missy . . . Beyond the time I woke up at the bottom of that cliff I *don't remember one goddam thing!*"

Her stare said she found that hard to take in. He could understand this, not yet having come to terms with it himself. "That's the God's own truth." He let out a bitter breath.

4

"You've no remembrance at all?"

He scowled at the jug, brought blue eyes up again like a man unused to accounting for himself. He lifted the jug to his cracked lips and swallowed.

"Look: I don't even know who I *am!*" he blurted.

"Then how did you know your name is Walt Parras?"

He peered irascibly and, tightening cracked lips, dug into the pocket of his shield-fronted shirt. "I *don't* know," he grumbled, and held out some grubby, rather dog-eared papers. "But if I ain't Parras what do you reckon I'm doing with these?"

The girl stayed where she was. Dark eyes watching narrowly, she left the whole burden of this thing up to him. She might be young but she was nobody's fool.

Opening one of the papers he held it up for her to see. "Transfer of horses made out to Walt Parras." He unfolded another. "Receipt for forty-five head of grade Hereford calves, also made out to Parras." He waved two more at her. "Couple of letters addressed to Parras care of General Delivery, Lordsburg."

She stood there in silence, aloof, uncommitted.

"Now," he growled, "you know as much as I do." He stared at her grimly. When it became obvious she'd no intention of saying more he put the papers away and, lifting a hand toward his rag-wrapped head, was making ready to leave when a sound of approaching hooves pulled him around to stare across the yard.

A huddle of horsemen swept in from the hills coming hellity-larrup to pull up in a dustcloud and a scatter of grit, the foremost less than six arm lengths away.

This was a Mexican in chin-strapped sombrero, swarthy and smiling below a pair of black eyes shiny as bottle glass and just as communicative. He had the full paunched shape of a prosperous ranchman.

Despite what she'd told him Parras thought this might be the mentioned Olivares. All the signs of a boss were there for the knowing. And while he gave the man closer attention a glance at the girl made it seem unlikely the man was her father. The age gap wasn't pronounced enough once you looked past that bristle of moustache.

The girl's words confirmed this. "Olivares," she said with evident relief, "this fellow's had an accident. In the dark last night his horse went over Tenkiller Cliff with him. Horse broke its neck and he's looking for work."

Back of Olivares several of the crew exchanged brow-lifted glances.

The ramrod's black stare hung reflectively on Parras. The girl said a little stiffly, "I suggested you could probably find something for him."

"Don Adolfo back from Socorro?"

Like a draft of cool air curling around his shoulders Parras felt the man's antagonism. A rift seemed to widen between this girl and her father's crew boss. Not anything you could put your finger on but definitely there and pretty plainly deepening.

The girl said coldly, "Not yet."

Olivares' black stare went over Parras again as a man might inspect something put up at auction. Parras might not be able to remember his past but enough trickled through from it to make him uncomfortable.

Olivares said, tone dubious, "You know how he feels about — "

"It would only be for a *little* while. The man's been hurt. He could surely stay till he's recovered his memory."

The ramrod's eyes sharpened. He got off his horse, tossing his reins to one of the crew. "Sit down, man. Get the weight off your feet." He watched Parras hobble around and lower himself to the sun-warped planks of the tacked-on porch. "How's that about your memory again?" He said in a kind of picked-over way, "You know who you are, don't you?"

Parras, shrugging, dug out the papers he'd unfolded for Teresa. The corpulent range boss, eyeing them briefly, passed them along to a rider behind him, a saddle-warped man with sun-peeled face who, peering, grunted, let them flutter away beneath the hooves of his mount.

Olivares said, "What do you make of this, Joel?"

The man's agate eyes quartered Parras' face with an open amusement, lips thin and crooked. "Saddle tramp drifter on the hunt for a handout."

In the bite of that triangular stare Parras pushed himself off the boards and got onto his feet. If he burned from this contempt it was nowhere apparent as, focusing on his tumble of papers, he bent by the horse in an awkward groping. Joel's grating voice said, "A gringo nobody — a nothing," derisively, and shoved him sprawling with the thrust of a boot.

The restive horse, jumping sideways, snorted. Parras lay for a bit, shuddering, groaning.

7

"No call for that, Fay," Olivares said mildly while they watched the downed man scrounge up onto a knee and hang fire on braced arms. "This feller ain't foolin'."

Parras, ignoring them, got hold of his papers, picked up his gun and stood painfully erect with no more animosity, Olivares decided, than you'd find in a sparrow. Fellow tried a couple times to stuff the gun in its holster, in the end pushing its barrel down inside his waistband. Peering about like a just woken sleepwalker he scrubbed the shaking hand — mud smeared from the broken olla — across stubbled cheeks.

The girl, flushed with anger, cried, "Get him over to the bunkhouse and leave him alone."

"But Don Adolfo — " the ramrod began when the girl chopped him off with one fierce look. "Don't translate my father to *me!* Do what I tell you, hombre — and take care of that wound. *Pronto!*"

The range boss did not look too happy about it but with what grace he could passed along her orders. Two vaqueros swung down but Parras shrugged them off with a growl. Ducking his head at the girl he set off on a floundering course across the yard. He took a dozen erratic steps and wound up flat on his face.

Olivares waved an arm and the men picked him up, going on past the corrals, disappearing into the bunkhouse with him.

Olivares chucked the girl a brief look. "Expect nothing of a dog beyond his hide."

CHAPTER
TWO

"Mr. Parras, this is my father, Don Adolfo Buenpaso de Romero y Cuencas . . . it might be that he can help you. Papa, this is the one I was telling you about, the man that went over Tenkiller Cliff."

Parras, swinging cramped legs to the floor, sat up somewhat dizzily and, peering out the west window, found the sun of another day pretty well down. He must have slept straight through. This tended to surprise him though he couldn't think why it should. Except for themselves the long bare room with its double row of bunks stood empty.

Even more astonished, he looked from Teresa to the old man beside her. At the grizzled cheeks corrugated as arroyos, the great beak of a nose with its broken red veins, the rheumy eyes and sunken hole of a mouth that kept opening and shutting with the vagaries of a jaw that seemed afflicted with ague.

It was hard to think how such a ruin could hope to be of much use to anyone. To Parras' questioning stare the man appeared — if not in his dotage — to be headed that way by the nearest route. His hands shook, too, his head as well. Brown spots large as ten-cent pieces decorated his face like overgrown freckles.

"Papa studied medicine in Mexico City," the girl threw in brightly as though by this to free Parras from his trance.

At least it roused him. He said with forced heartiness he was powerfully pleased to make the acquaintance of so distinguished a gentleman, and assured the old man his largesse had not been strewn before swine. "I'm no charity case; I'll want to work for my keep."

The old man's rheumy stare traveled over his daughter, brightening briefly between waist and throat while she explained a bit dryly: "He wants to repay you."

Don Adolfo said "How?" and Parras, catching an irony he hadn't expected, had the grace to flush a little.

"Up to you to say that. Expect I could make out to say on a horse."

Don Adolfo did not appear greatly interested. Waving his arms he declared irascibly that he had more vaqueros than he had dollars. "Perhaps," Teresa ventured, "he could break some of those young colts for you. Which would leave Bartolo free to attend — "

The old man waved that away as irrelevant. "Madigan and Yorba are fixing to roundup," she tucked in, plainly determined. "Joel didn't get on too well with them last time. Perhaps if you sent an Anglo to represent us we would have less trouble with these gringo neighbors."

Her father jerked up his head like a bot fly had struck him. Almost seemed for a moment as he might once have looked in the days when he was putting this outfit together. But this sharpness of spirit only served to remind one of the ravages of time, wizzling away to leave him, as before, the futile victim of capricious ill humor.

In a petulant wheeze he grumblingly demanded, "Does the gopher make friends of the snake and the buzzard? You speak of men's business, girl. We have to send someone who'll take up for our rights, a man who is just as unprincipled as they are. Olivares understands what makes these Texicans tick."

But the girl couldn't keep her mouth shut. "I doubt," she said with a curl of the lip, "he's greatly concerned about what is best for the Romeros. Some day when they're here you'd better look at your crew and see how many faces you remember."

The old man scowled. Teresa's angry eyes flashed. "And who will you be leaving this ranch to — Olivares?"

The old man's cheeks stiffened, darkly affronted. "Go to your room. I won't be talked to like that."

The girl tossed her chin. "How does Olivares talk to you, Papa? With honeyed words dripping off that forked tongue, or does he lay down the orders with a lifted pistol?"

The old man, shaking, stalked off in a pet.

Parras asked gruffly, "Wasn't that being kind of rough on him?"

"Olivares doesn't fool *me!*" she cried fiercely. "I can see what he's up to! He has dreams of the peon becoming the patron but he's not going to get away with it, I tell you!"

11

Parras said, not entirely joshing, "You ever been told how much anger becomes you?" and saw the bright color it put in her cheeks. She bit her lip in annoyance but it was true enough, he thought. With those flashing eyes, chin up like a stallion, not many would pass her without looking back.

Flattery, it seemed, only prodded the distrust in her. Nervously darting a look toward the house, as though coming to a decision, she abruptly asked, "Do you feel much like riding?"

"What's that got to do with the price of cabbages?"

"Ca-bagges? Oh, I see . . . a gringo joke," she said, looking nettled. "You think, like my father, I am just a foolish girl." She pulled up her chin, declaring, "No matter! You expressed a wish to work for your keep — was that intended to be funny, too?"

She was so goddam earnest about everything he couldn't be sure how he ought to take this. She might just be right about Olivares fixing to take over. This looked a pretty good setup for that sort of caper. Place wasn't being kept up like it ought to be; the tattletale signs of neglect were plain. But how was this any concern of his?

"What do you want me to do?" he said finally.

"You could turn up at Roman Four as our strayman."

"And what happens then if Joel Fay shows?"

"Are you afraid of that halfbreed?"

With such an excess of scorn he wondered what she was setting him up for. "I've only seen the man once,"

12

he countered. "If he should turn up I wouldn't be left with much authority, would I?"

"That would probably depend on how you handled things. You'd be working for me — I could give you a note . . ."

Parras didn't much like the look of any part of going in there cold with a note from a woman. But he *did* owe her something. The food he had eaten, the use of this bunk, had certainly not come through any kindness of Joel Fay's boss, Olivares. "But won't your father — "

Teresa said, shaking her head, "He is most of the time in his room with a bottle. I break all I find, but . . . We have this ranch — on paper, at least — but its control is managed on orders that come from Olivares. You see, it's not Papa's way to seek advice from a woman."

"And how did Olivares get into such clover?"

"My father has not been well. All I know is what I see. New faces everywhere. I don't know if you're aware of this but most Spanish properties are not worked by their owners but are managed on the mayordomo system."

"You're tellin' me, I guess, that Olivares does just about as he pleases."

"Olivares," she said bitterly, "is my father's Trojan horse."

"And how did he fall heir to this job?"

Teresa shrugged and her lips were tight. "I have not been told. Eladio Gomez was in the position when this ranch came to Papa on the death of his father. A fall from a horse killed Gomez three years ago. Olivares came then."

"If he was not on your payroll when Gomez took that fall somebody must have recommended him. Man just doesn't ride up to a spread and get straightaway settled in the top screw's job."

"I believe the bank vouched for him."

"*What* bank?"

"The bank at Socorro which handles our accounts. They gave him, my father says, a very good character."

"Be interesting to know how much that cost him," Parras said dryly. "How much of your paper is that bank carrying?"

You could see she didn't like it. Her chin climbed resentfully and her pansy-colored eyes showed the arrogance bred into her.

"Favors," Parras mentioned, "usually beget favors. If you expect anything from me speak up."

"My father speaks only to Olivares of such things."

"Who runs that bank?"

"Sig MacGurdy."

"A *norteamericano?*"

"A gringo, certainly," she said with her sullen eyes turning disdainful.

"Yeah," Parras said with some scorn of his own. "I take it your father doesn't care much for Anglos. How big is this spread?"

She studied the planes of his cheeks, undecided. Said at last with a shrug, "It was a grant from the Spanish Crown to Don Esteban, my grandfather. From a point on the Rio Grande so many *varas* south of Elephante

14

Butte one full day's ride in any direction; I doubt that it's ever been measured exactly."

Parras, shaking his head at the prodigality of kings and the carelessness of *rícos*, looked disgusted. "And where does your neighbor Madigan do his banking?"

"At Socorro. It's closer, you see. You have to go around the mountains to get to El Paso."

"Sounds quite a busy place. He keeping his nest egg under MacGurdy?"

"There is just the one bank."

A fine kettle of fish, Parras thought. Of course *norteamericanos* — unlike Mexicans — did not always hang together, and more especially Texicans. But with a ranch like this up for grabs — and it probably was — there didn't seem much doubt which side MacGurdy's bank would be throwing its weight with.

"All right," Parras growled. "Write your note and I'll drift over there."

CHAPTER
THREE

Having gotten directions, some forty minutes later he was on his way aboard a handsome bay gelding that looked to have been bred to both bottom and speed. Playing strayman rep at the Madigan roundup should provide a reason for remaining in this neighborhood until he got back enough of his memory to discover what purpose had brought him to the base of a cliff alongside a horse that had been shot out from under him.

He was much more concerned about this than any possible run-in he might have with Joel Fay. Hired guns, as a rule, were not prone to press their luck without the advantage of an obvious edge, which was one thing Parras didn't intend to provide. Not if keeping his eyes peeled had anything to do with it.

In searching his clothes to find out who he was he had discovered, buttoned into one of his shirt pockets, close to two hundred dollars in folding money, which seemed a bit much to be packing around under normal circumstances. It suggested he was here on some sort of mission but he couldn't imagine any use for such a sum that made very much sense.

The only halfway likely thing he could think of was that he'd come to this region on a horse buying trip, but this did not seem a heap likely. Even at bargain prices a man couldn't buy such a much for two hundred, yet it was too fat a roll for a chuckline rider. And if he'd lived around here some of this crew should have recognized him.

If they had, it had not been evident.

The two letters addressed to Parras at Lordsburg didn't appear overburdened with information. Neither of them mentioned this ranch or Madigan, or anything else that looked like being helpful. And if he'd lived around Lordsburg they wouldn't have been sent to General Delivery.

One, from a man signing himself Farnol, asked him to drop by Shakespeare at early convenience and get in touch with an Idewall Jones, but the letter had been dated April 6, and if a man was to go by what he saw around him it was considerably closer right now to October. Just the same, he thought grimly, if the past stayed a blank and he couldn't get a lead any other way it might just pay him to take a ride over there.

The other letter offered even less in its ambiguity. Dated April 2, it said: *Think our friend, for whatever it's worth, has smelled a mouse and dug for the tules.* The only thing resembling a signature was the *M* tacked after this cryptic remark. It had been mailed from Dos Cabezas.

He got no help out of that. If ever he'd heard of the place he'd forgotten it. Lordsburg was south of here a couple hundred miles. He marveled that he should be so certain of this. He could see it against the blank of his mind, a one-street town that — except for the yellow painted railroad property — was mostly deadfalls and gambling dives.

Still thinking about those letters he got to wondering if he was some kind of a lawman. A deputy marshal might get that sort of mail. But so might a man on the dodge, and a lawman had ought to have some kind of badge . . . he didn't have to have, though. Texas Rangers did a lot of moving about without badges but it did not seem likely they'd be operating here. Still, they might if the mission was urgent enough . . . following someone they'd been told to fetch back.

He shook off his dark thoughts to consider this Madigan. If the fellow was laying pipe to take over the Romero spread it didn't seem probable he'd be advertising the fact. Olivares, if he was crooked, was in far better shape as the outfit's ramrod to take over the ranch than any outsider even with a bank or a mortgage behind him.

If paper was being carried on the Two-Pole Pumpkin it was almost certain to be in the hands of the banker, MacGurdy. There were several situations which might have forced Don Adolfo into borrowing on his holdings — drought, a poor market, the inroads of rustlers, a weakness for cards or some other form of gambling. The old man didn't strike Parras as a particularly robust character.

There were plenty of signs of neglect, of poor management, though. If Don Adolfo, as the girl had so bitterly claimed, spent most of his time locked away with a bottle, Olivares was in good shape to do just as he pleased.

Big trouble, of course, with the most of this figuring was the dependence it put on what the girl had come out with. You had to recollect she had a chip on her shoulder.

If you could believe what she said — and he was a long way from sure it would be smart to swallow all of it — the cause of her antagonism was no great mystery.

With her kind of looks this place would seem a prison. To be chained to the spread with a half senile father watching that big-gutted ramrod making more and more use of the owner's prerogatives, setting himself up as the final authority . . . It was really no wonder she looked fit to be tied; or that, in her rebellion, she would seize any stick that came to hand.

She might not be a day over eighteen — girl's ages weren't too easy to hit on — but it was all too evident she wasn't getting any younger. Most *ricos*' daughters were married at her age with a home of their own and umpteen servants to play the lady with. She was bound to be desperate at the trend things were taking, her heritage being usurped by one who was no better than a scheming hired hand. If she was right.

He guessed she might, with a little persuasion, be willing to run away with him. Other girls, he reckoned, had tried that with a lot less provocation. Love was the operative word and easily spoken. These hidalgos were traditionally pretty strict with their women. A daughter's marriage was arranged for benefits accruing. Seldom was a girl's opinion sought or given weight.

Parras blew out his cheeks in exasperation. He had problems enough of his own right now. For all he knew he might already be married with half a dozen kids . . . He didn't feel like he was and sure as hell hoped not; he didn't feel like the kind who would want to be tied down — but he found it hard just the same to put this girl out of mind. A man didn't run into her kind too often. Even this far away he could feel the pull of her . . . the way she wrinkled her nose up and the fit of that bodice across the top half of her.

He tried to concentrate on Fay, what the man was like to do if he came out to that roundup and found Parras installed as rep for Two-Pole Pumpkin. Would Joel act without orders?

Parras' glance stretched out across the dusty hills, hunting landmarks the girl had mentioned. Turn west to the river, Teresa had told him. He wouldn't see any river from where he was now. The lemon grass waved ahead in a series of rolls separated by ridges into independent valleys. He was crossing one now, presently climbing through pungent crests of pine that cut down vision until the horse rimmed out and he saw blue water ahead of him.

That blue was deceptive, an illusion created by heat and light and the immensity of sky with its tatter of clouds all puffed up in white swirls like the towering sails of a fleet of square-riggers. When he came upon the near bank, the river was the color of coffee laced with cream. He could see flood marks high upon the far wall but had no way of gauging how deep the current ran.

He didn't like the look of it and rode north a spell in search of a better crossing. Didn't look like there'd been any rain here in months but he'd no desire to find himself swimming; he kept on until he came to a discernible trail turning down the cut bank and saw the low hump of the hill which Teresa had told him marked the freighters' ford.

He crossed without mishap, the water coming only half-way up his stirruped boots. According to the girl he was now on Roman Four, Madigan's spread.

Ten minutes later he saw the distant shapes of riders and swung that way, uneasily wondering what kind of reception he was letting himself in for.

A small browsing herd was being held by a pair of circle-riding hands and off beyond, maybe half a mile, he saw the outfit's wagon. The nearest rider, as Parras approached, waved him around and sat a moment looking after him as Parras cut over to come up to the camp.

The stove-up cook didn't show too friendly but answered Parras' hail with a reticent nod. Parras stopped his horse but stayed in the saddle. "I'm looking," he said, "for the Roman Four wagon."

The cook under lowering brows eyed him darkly. "You figurin' to work or just lookin' for a handout?"

CHAPTER
FOUR

"What I'm looking for mostly," Parras said, "is a boss," and slewed a quick glance across the half dozen horses picketed close by. All Roman Fours; but as his half-turned head swiveled back toward the dough wrangler he caught a sound of ridden horses coming up from the left and coosie allowed, "You won't have t' git out your night clothes then. Unless my eyes has gone plumb back on me that's him comin' yonder."

Parras backed his mount off a bit to take in the newcomers without leaving the cook outside his perspective. Coosie curled his lip at this but Parras, not overlooking the man's sour humor, was considerably more engrossed with the pair riding toward him.

They both looked like bosses but it did not take any great amount of study to make out which was which. The one nearest as they pulled up had the indefinable air of an owner, with his pantslegs stuffed into boots you couldn't buy off a shelf and a flat-topped black hat half hiding the stab of his miss-nothing glance. He put together a smoke, which he stuck on the lip of a long horsey face while, not bothering to light it, he looked Parras over.

It was the other rider though that hemmed Parras in with a splatter of questions. They came from the belligerent look of his face with the sarcastic impact of a tax collector's challenge. Parras answered the gist of them by inquiring, "This *is* the Roman Four wagon, isn't it?"

The horse-faced man, giving back a cool look, inclined his head but the man with the questions wasn't leaving it there. He said in a harsh attacking sort of snarl: "You got a bill of sale for that horse you're forking?"

"I don't see," Parras said, "that it's any of your business."

The man, probably Madigan's range boss, showed the color of anger. He was big — even bigger than Parras — with a muscular swell of chest and arm that would have seemed quite at home in the hide of an elephant. Bold and lively features showed a spread of yellowed teeth as he shifted his chaw from one cheek to the other. He was a sandy-haired man with lips long and rimless and the arrogant stare of a man who hadn't been crossed in a considerable while. But before he could talk himself into a corner the black-hatted man said with an easy indifference, "I quite agree. My name is Madigan," and held out a hand.

Leaning out from the saddle Parras warily shook it. "Walt Parras," he murmured. "I've come to join your crew as rep for the Romeros."

The sandy-haired coot, bold eyes half shut, demanded: "Why would they send *you?*" and, not waiting for an answer, growled in disbelieving tone, "What's the matter with Joel?"

"Expect you'll have to ask him about that." Parras, producing the girl's note and straightening the leg that was in the near stirrup, held the paper out to Madigan.

The rancher, unfolding it, tipped his head a little forward. He must have gone through it twice before, pulling up his chin, he coolly asked, "Fay coming, too?"

"I haven't been taken into Fay's confidence."

The rancher stared without saying anything. "Funny," he grumbled finally, rasping a hand the length of his jaw. "Always before it's been Fay that repped for them. Did the old man give you this chore himself?"

"It was the girl sent me over. Seemed to figure it might take less time and be more satisfactory if Joel didn't stand in for Two-Pole Pumpkin at this cow hunt."

Parras did not miss the looks that flashed between the pair of them. Madigan's glance, coming back, showed a freshening interest. "How long you been working for the Romeros, Parras?"

"That has something to do with this?"

Smiling wryly Madigan let it go. "Did Olivares hire you?"

"He's the ramrod over there, ain't he?"

"I expect," Madigan said, "you find this all kind of queer. It's simple enough when you understand the personalities involved. Yorba, my foreman," he explained with a slanchways look in his companion's direction, "once had a hankering for the job Olivares got — that was before he got made top screw here. Mostly they

24

manage to ignore each other, but ever since Yorba caught on at Roman Four they been sending that hired pistolero to rep at our roundups. You might almost say they been askin' for trouble."

Parras, saying nothing, sat waiting politely.

With a reticent shrug Madigan said, "Yorba's in charge. You'll take your orders from him."

He got out of his saddle and, dropping the reins, stepped over to the wagon, poured a mug full of java. With this cupped in his hands he surveyed Parras again.

Yorba told Parras: "You go help those boys ridin' circle," and got off his own horse to stride toward the tail gate.

Parras rode toward the herd without looking back. On any beef roundup there'd be more men involved than he had seen up to now. The rest of them likely were still hunting cows, combing the cedar brakes, some of them probably searching the draws of those flat-topped hills he could see in the distance. The sun was just about down but they'd be kept at this work for as long as there was any light left to see by.

This hunting of "windies" was no work for an amateur. They were generally contrary and difficult to drive and by the time they were gotten to a holding ground everyone concerned was usually pretty much exhausted, hence the name.

Cattle, by and large, were inclined to remain on territory to which they had become accustomed, the home range. But there were always some which ranged further afield, prone to seek other places to water, expecting browse elsewhere to be more to their liking. These bunch-quitter cattle became strays and sooner or eventually mixed with the other folks' critters, which forced the various brands to hire regular straymen or, more frequently, to dispatch reps to neighboring roundups. Rangeland, in those days, was not sufficiently crowded to bring about the later innovation of district roundups. In this time and place each outfit held its own.

Quite a number of miscellaneous facts were joggling around in Parras' head as he joined the pair lazily circling the herd. There were things coming back to him or never forgotten which suggested familiarity with this kind of work. The two circling Roman Four riders rode in opposite directions.

Parras exchanged casual nods with the first hand he came to, not giving the fellow any great amount of attention, waiting where he'd stopped until a sufficient interval extended between them before butting his gelding into the man's wake. But when the second rider passed him Parras' eyes narrowed thoughtfully, this being a different type entirely: gaunt enough to get through the eye of a needle, with the burned powder smell of gunman about him. Danger crouched in the slant of warped features, his bony shape string thin where he jogged hunched over the butt of a pistol secured by his waistband for easy reaching.

Parras considered the thought of this fellow being Madigan's answer to Joel Fay. It would depend of course on how long he had been here. If he wasn't a new hand a different explanation would have to be looked for, like Fay's being imported by Olivares as a defensive measure against possible aggression. Cow outfits in the normal course of events did not employ pistoleros without they were in trouble or had reason to expect it.

Counties were large, law officers scarce and resident deputies in places that had them were not always able to withstand the pressures. The more Parras turned these things over in his mind the better he understood that girl reaching out to him. Must have felt pretty desperate to find hope in a stranger.

CHAPTER
FIVE

Teresa *was* desperate — very near ready to start climbing walls. A Mexican national apparently forgotten in a land taken over by pushy aliens, in a very real and lately frightening sense she was discovering herself — though not even yet fully able to believe this — a prisoner. In the calmer moments she spent trying to pin down this outrageous conviction it seemed preposterously fantastic, figment almost of a disarranged mind.

There were no visible constraints, nothing one could actually touch or see with the suddenness of a jerked-around stare, but she was as surely chained to the echoing mockery of this isolated hacienda as the adobe bricks plastered into the three-foot thickness of its moldering walls. As trapped as her flighty half crazy father drinking himself into sodden oblivion behind locked doors. Caught in the strands of the cunning web being spun by that fat grinning spider, Polito Olivares, so smugly usurping the prerogatives of owner.

In more rational moments she found the whole thing absurd, yet this did little to erode the creeping terror that was like two hands closing around her throat. She was strangely afraid of him, even more afraid than she was of Joel Fay, who had also, apparently, begun to nurse notions of a closer proximity.

She could understand Fay, who was crudely obnoxious, but the cat and mouse game Olivares was engaged in was in all of its components too elusive, too slyly derisive, to furnish anything you could wrap around a post and hold for prolonged scrutiny.

When he wasn't on tap in person there was always someone available with a glib excuse or a flint-hard stare to turn her back from any hope of a horse. If she set off by herself to move outside the yard she was either caught up with or casually followed with such cool assurance no one but an idiot could fail to understand.

The man had never put a hand on her but she had sensed the lecherous thinking behind the salacious mockery so frequently glinting from his fat toad's stare. His designs on the property had lately been enlarged to incorporate her person and it was this, much as anything, which had turned her so concernedly frantic.

Prior to the advent of this gringo, Parras, there'd been no one she could turn to. She had at one panicked point even considered with trembling reluctance encouraging a breach between Olivares and his pistolero, but that would have only swapped the witch for a devil she instinctively knew would be like an animal in his unbridled lust.

Yet . . . if she worked Parras right . . .

If she played her cards properly and the man proved as tough as he had looked to her that morning . . . It was something, at least, a person could get on with after so many days of frustrated inaction, and if he should take care of Fay, who would almost inevitably be dispatched to that cow hunt, there seemed a *chance* at any rate he might tie into Olivares or at least be maneuvered into taking her away from here.

None of these notions were etched that graphically in her thinking; it was just that she'd been ripe to latch onto almost anything and this fellow was available. She wasn't about to lean much weight on him. It was pretty long odds he'd show up at that roundup or appreciably help if he did, but at least she had finally put something in motion.

"About this guy Parras . . . " Madigan said to his range boss. "What you reckon that outfit's up to sending this cottonmouth over to rep for them?"

"I dunno," Yorba grunted. "Might not be so rough as he looks. What was the sense of that paper he give you?"

"Just a note from the girl suggesting he came with the old man's blessin'. You think they've got onto us?"

"That damn Olivares ain't no easy one to figger." Yorba scowled at a fist and slapped it down on the horn. "I wouldn't be trustin' him farther'n I could throw him."

Madigan scowled too, rasping a hand across his scraggle of whiskers. "We know the bastard likes money or we couldn't have set this up."

"Mebbe he's found some slicker way, some deal that don't cut his profits in half."

"Well, he *could* be figuring to go after the whole loaf. You think this Parras is a sure enough gun hawk?"

Yorba shrugged. "Mebbe we oughta flip a line out to Joel."

Madigan considered and said, tone thoughtful, "If they're taking on more guns they're certainly up to something. If they're fixing to cut us out of this deal it ought to be apparent in pretty short order."

"How's all this goin' to set with MacGurdy?"

"It ain't like to make him very all-fired happy."

"How much of Romero's debt has that Yank sold you?"

Madigan rubbed his chin with the heel of a hand. "Presumbably all of it — I got no way of knowing."

"If he's holdin' out couldn't that make things kinda sticky? You've sunk quite a passel in them notes, ain't you, boss? If the old man fails to make that next payment an' you bring in the sheriff an' take him over you could be in bad shape with that banker for a pardner."

Madigan said gruffly, "Bankers can have accidents same as anybody else."

Meanwhile, back at Two-Pole Pumpkin, Olivares, returning with his work weary crew, spun a look about the yard and with his words slapping out like pistol shots told his troubleshooter to roust out Parras on the double. Letting go of his reins, leaving the horse to be put up by one of his lackeys, the corpulent self-made boss jangled through the main gate and disappeared into one of the rooms off the patio.

A desk, cheek by jowl with a brass-posted bed, had been crowded into this room when the man took it over. Unlocking the desk — an old battered rolltop — he dug out a bottle, upending it into his thrown-back head, sloshing a mouthful of the fiery contents around through his teeth before driving the cork into the neck of it.

He was just setting it down when Fay came dragging his spurs across the parquet. "Can't find him," the gunhand grumbled, reaching out for the bottle.

Olivares, scowling, knocked his hand away. "Maybe you better go look again."

"He's gone," Fay said, "and that big chestnut, too."

The ramrod's black stare went opaquely still. Fay said with the lift of a lip corner: "If you want my notion he's pulled his freight."

Olivares ignored this. A thin sweat appeared at either side of his nose. "Did you see the girl?"

Fay said sullenly, "She's in her room."

"Get her over here."

When the man went off Olivares took another pull at the bottle. He had a pretty good hunch where Parras had got to and the conviction did nothing to improve his humor. When Fay returned, tagging after Teresa, Olivares said to her, "Your father won't like this," and saw her flush.

His own face darkened when she stood there silently, her stare filled with open defiance.

He was riled enough to strike her; one hand half lifted before he got hold of his rampaging temper. He let the hand drop and, waving her away, settled the length of his black stare on Fay when that leering womanizer forced the girl to squeeze past him getting out of the room.

Although his grim stare held the man in its compass the foreman's thoughts had little room and less inclination to be tied up with any matter so negligible as paid pistoleros.

He had more substantial worries. Tough ones like Parras could be astonishingly naïve, preposterously maneuverable, when it came to obliging a good-looking filly. Teresa, of course, wouldn't know this. It wasn't hard to guess — without any money — what she had thought up to offer that gringo.

He let her steps die away still skewering Fay with that broken-off regard.

As mayordomo of this place Oliveres had ways of keeping in touch with what went on, but he needed to know one thing above all right now: whether or not this gringo was faking . . . and who could tell him that?

Not this gun. Not the girl or her *borracho* father who no longer had any outside contact except by the grace of Polito Olivares. True, he had allowed the old fool to go with trusted men as far off as Socorro periodically — how else could he have gotten cash money to pay the hands? And that was something to laugh about, too.

He didn't look like laughing when he remembered the appearance of this unshaven gringo. And it was more than just physical impressions, that bulldog jaw. Polito might not know enough about the fellow to form a proper basis for predicting probabilities but he knew considerably more than he'd intention of revealing. He had an old and proved remedy for things that got too deeply into his hair . . . but there was more to this than Parras.

He hadn't rightly glimpsed the danger in Romero's trips to Socorro; now, so grimly reminded of Madigan, the corridors of his thinking were blackly alive with apprehensions.

Those payrolls — which Olivares had been pocketing — were secured on loans from MacGurdy, in support of which the girl's father signed over certain specified numbers of Romero branded cattle . . . many of which could no longer be found should the bank make a search to count up its collateral.

It was the mayordomo's deal with Madigan which had so drastically tampered with the status quo. Until Parras had come riding onto the scene it had not occurred to Romero's range boss there would be any likelihood of the two schemes colliding. Even if Parras had no connection with the bank, with him loose on the range engaged as a strayman he could hardly fail to note a discrepancy between the girth of the brand and the amount of steers marked with it.

Something would have to be managed very quickly. Safest thing was to kill the damned gringo.

This could be engineered, he thought, eyeing the gunfighter.

He passed over the bottle, watching good whiskey run down the man's throat. When Fay came up for air Olivares murmured suggestively: "It's plain Teresa sent our friend to that cow hunt to look into what's happening to that stock we've been missing. Sent him over there to rep for us." When Fay's lifting face scowled the mayordomo said, "You got any notions?" like it had him stumped.

The gunfighter's pale stare swiveled and slitted like the eyes of a snake and he growled from a mouth corner, "You want I should go over there?"

"Not if you don't feel up to it. You've always *been* our rep with that outfit . . . You think that hombre could be working for the bank? That guff about him going over Tenkiller — sound reasonable to you? Pretty much of a drop for a man to walk away from." The range boss prodded. "He seem like to you the kind of fool that would mislay his memory?"

The gunslinger was plainly beginning to squirm. Like most pistoleros Fay, vain of his prowess, was easily affronted. Pride was a thing his kind set great store by and, using this knowledge, Olivares said with a tinge of derision, "If you don't figure you can handle — "

Fay, head snapping up, snarled: "Who said I couldn't handle him?" His belligerent stare gleamed like broken glass, a darkening color angrily brightening his cheeks. "You want him took care of just say so!"

"No skin off *my* nose. If MacGurdy's steered him onto this spread it's not *me* the law is going to come down on. It was you set up that business with Madigan. *I* didn't help run off those critters. If that feller's come in here to make a count it's you and that Madigan outfit, I'd say, that's got the real worry of whatever comes out of this."

Fay's eyes had slimmed down to glittering slits. "Alls I've got out of it has been day wages!"

Olivares smiled. "Kind of hard thing to prove."

"Madigan knows who got half that money!"

"Might think he does but you're the one he paid it to." The mayordomo showed a bland face. On the edge of a smile he said, discouragingly confident, "Be just your word against mine. If you don't want to find yourself fitted for hemp you better take care of this before it gets down to that."

CHAPTER
SIX

Fay didn't like it. Not the least part of it, but that twister's fist was wrapped in his short hairs where the least little twitch could do him grave injury.

All the while the gunfighter was saddling he sidled around the notion of putting a slug where it would do the most good. He had killed for less and probably would again but you just didn't eliminate an egg-laying goose while there was maybe a chance of getting more eggs out of it.

Slamming into the saddle, he tore out of the yard like a blue-tailed fly.

Perhaps he didn't grasp all the ramifications but he was bright enough to have a good hunch what that son of a bitch Olivares was up to!

By all the signs and signal-smokes Olivares was figuring to take this brand over. And the way things shaped up the odds sure as hell were stacked in his favor. Nobody saw the old Don hardly ever and — because of the drifters prowling these hills — it was expressly forbidden to let the girl on a horse unless amply accompanied by men hand-picked by the range boss himself. These were orders and there wasn't nobody going to risk disobeying them. Not with that kind of guy to account to!

Uncomfortable things frequently caught up with persons running counter to the boss man's notions. Fay recalled a number of examples. You might discount some but a man did not replace a whole crew without there were things he wanted kept hidden.

The turning over of his thoughts wore away the sharper edge of Fay's more obvious ferment but a core of frustrated fury continued to smolder far back in his stare. No one but a fool would shrug and turn another cheek to a vinegarroon cold-blooded enough to smilingly point out the kind of bind he'd put you in.

Why was Olivares so disturbed about this saddlebum? The country was crawling with masterless gringos a lot meaner looking than this hombre Parras. What was so special about him, Fay wondered, that he had to be removed in such an all-fired hurry?

Reason given might be truth and plenty adequate but it hardly appeared sufficiently urgent to maneuver Olivares into such a brash disclosure.

Fay's thoughts boiled around this for the next couple miles and the more he looked at it the more likely it seemed the mayordomo had some special purpose carefully hugged to his gizzard. Man might almost imagine there was something personal back of it.

With sharpening stare Fay's thoughts, taking a jump, swiveled around to the girl, the old Don's daughter. A juicy piece sure enough, and Fay had seen the range boss looking her over.

If Olivares could get her into double harness it would go a great ways toward consolidating his position. Almost certainly it was Teresa who'd sent Parras to Roman Four. The girl was afraid of Olivares — Fay had seen too much to doubt this. Afraid but still defiant . . .

If the bastard could take Parras out of this picture it might well pull the last rug from under her.

And where had Olivares been the night that gringo went over Tenkiller?

Parras, combing the brakes with three other hands, didn't have much leisure for examining his problems. This was hard grueling work filled with peril and danger even to men who had been raised on this terrain. There were rocks in this brush half concealed — sometimes wholly, and one moment of carelessness could get a man killed or crippled so badly he might wish he was.

The purpose of these cow hunts independently staged by the various outfits was multi-faceted: the chance for a count during this gathering-up; a sorting out — the stuff to be sold and the critters kept for growth and breeding; the branding of all, young or old, that had no mark of ownership burned onto them; an opportunity to observe the inroads of rustlers, and the chance for other owners to reclaim strayed stock.

These affairs had not yet become carefully planned or generally organized. They were small local works rather loosely conducted and not very systematic, more in the nature of neighborhood frolics, seldom covering any great amount of country.

You had to remember this was unfenced range, a free grass operation where larger outfits generally took precedence, chousing smaller operations off into places where water was hard to come by. Men might accept this but cattle, by and large, generally moved toward places they could slake their thirst; this rather frequently mixed up the brands, a fact of the business which all too often festered into open strife.

Parras wondered if the dissatisfaction hinted at between Olivares' crew and this Roman Four outfit had at least part of its roots in friction engendered by an overlapping of range. Other things aside this mule-voiced Madigan didn't have the look of being easy to get along with, and also to be weighed was Don Adolfo's inclination to regard all gringos as a pack of thieves and robbers.

Obviously he'd been around before Madigan's advent, another facet which scarcely tended to improve the situation.

The Roman Four owner, like many another with cattle baron leanings, had the hungry look of a man on the make, the sort of opportunist all too frequently met with in the reconstruction years following Lee's defeat at Richmond. Madigan might not have a carpetbag but he showed most of the proclivities of that sort of jasper: the bullypuss kind who liked to throw his weight about.

This was the beef roundup Madigan was engaged in; its most important priority was the assembling of cattle destined for market, and the branding of any late calves. Generally this was done with more deliberation than the spring gather, which was concerned directly with branding the increase. The animals now were heavier in flesh and every pound knocked off would be reflected in the price, though you might not have guessed this watching those mossyhorns being snaked from the brush. The range boss, Yorba, appeared a deal more concerned with the size of the gather than he did with its condition.

Parras found himself becoming more and more puzzled by the nervous energy with which Yorba drove them. You might almost have thought it was a race against time. When this gather was finished and they were through with the branding there would still be the drive to the railroad ahead of them. It was Roman Four's custom to ship from Lordsburg, but even if they hoped to be first to the market it didn't make sense to chouse these critters like a bunch of fool yahoos.

Another thing found odd was the way Yorba broke up the crew into segments, with never less than three or four working as a unit. There were six hands here from other outfits and never two reps in any one segment. It was late in Parras' second day with this outfit before he discovered this and began looking around.

It just about had to be deliberate, but what was its purpose? Had to be more than a Yankee's desire to get a full day out of neighboring helpers. Insurance against trouble?

Might be something to that but what sort of trouble would be like to erupt that could suggest such a caution of a hard nose like Yorba? There had been no discernible effort last night to keep these loan riders from getting together.

All the strayed brands were thrown into one bunch kept apart from the main hold composed of Roman Four cattle. The reps, he'd noticed, had been told off in pairs to keep this smaller jag from mixing with the others. A natural enough choice but it did nevertheless shrink the number of outsiders the wagon boss had to keep an eye out for.

The only thing Parras hit on for sure was the feeling of tension hanging over this crew, and it seemed to be mounting with each passing hour. The day rolled along filled with sweat and confusion and the Romero rep was on his fourth horse when he discovered the Roman Four gunhand inspecting him across the sprawled shape of a just-roped cow.

She had a full bag but no calf in sight; a hobbling gait was what had caused Parras to forefoot her. It was plain enough now that her two front feet had been burned between the toes with a hot piece of iron.

Parras shook off his loop and the cow lunged erect. While he was reeling in and coiling his twine the Roman Four hand with a bony look said, "Kinda seems some waddy's been makin' a orphan."

Wells was this fellow's handle; the hands called him Indigo. Parras returned the man's look with feigned indifference. "Damn sure wasn't this waddy," he said coolly, flipping the onus of decision back to Wells. Because the man's stare got under his hide Parras pushed it a couple breaths further, quietly asking, "You figuring to put this onto me, mister?"

Wells did not seem to much like the tone of that but, making an irritable shift of his weight, growled, "Don't yell till you're stepped on," and, yanking his horse around, sent it pelting after the cow, pushing the hot-foot on toward a number of grazing others recently jumped from this patch of brush.

The other two hands that had been working this draw sat their kaks with unnaturally blank faces, carefully avoiding the Romero rep's stare.

The sun didn't look more than half a dozen inches from dropping out of sight and, though Parras' gut felt pretty well tied in knots, he judged they wouldn't be heading for the wagon as long as there was light still left to swing a rope by. Wells, coming back, confirmed this impression, waving them off toward the draw's far wall, a slope heavily grown to juniper and buck brush. "See if you can comb anything outa there."

It was slow, rough going trying to force a way through that tangle of chaparral. The leather chaps worn by Parras' companions fended the thorns with a minimum of anguish. Not having this advantage, Parras maneuvered into the lead, found himself faring not much better than his whickering horse.

They didn't jump a thing from that devilish brasada and, time they rimmed out on the crest of the spur, Parras felt like he had taken about all he could and started looking around for a better way back.

It was still fairly light on the spine of this ridge though the area they'd left was half buried in shadow. Standing up in the stirrups he was raking this gloom when something zinged past with the whine of a hornet. Parras heard the flat crack of a distant rifle as he flung up a leg and departed the saddle.

CHAPTER
SEVEN

Parras hit the ground rolling, one hand fisting his rifle, but nothing further happened; when he popped up his head there was nothing to look at but that dark stretch of brush they had just climbed out of and, beyond perhaps another couple hundred yards, the far side of this coulee with nothing showing there either, not even the smudge of black powdersmoke.

A swiveled stare at his companions suggested no collusion; they appeared as disconcerted as he had been himself. "What the hell was that for?" the freckled one grumbled, peering somewhat edgily into those yonder coagulated shadows. "You see anythin', Deuce?"

The other limb-skinner shook his tow head. Getting back into the saddle Parras said shortly, "Let's get out of here," and led off across the spine of high ground in a catercornering fashion that put considerable growth between their watchful progress and the gloom-shrouded trough all three of them distrusted.

The cow Parras had tumbled carried the brand of Madigan's outfit, which might account in part for the string-thin Indigo's bristly attitude but did not, by even the most partisan reckoning, justify throwing lead. Yet who but Wells had been over that way?

44

It wasn't the kind of caper a man could put comfortably out of his mind, nor could Parras, with all the good will in the world, attribute a near miss like that to fidgety temper. If Madigan had reason for begrudging his presence it might have been figured the Romero strayman would have second thoughts about staying on where a blue whistler whipped past his cheek whispering *cousin*.

There were too many if's in this pie to suit Parras.

On the far side of the spur they slid onto low ground and worked their way gingerly through more brush to come out with two steers in the thickening shadows some half a mile east of where they'd left Wells. Here they jumped up three more and, hazing these along with the other pair, set off for the site of the held herds and wagon.

Deuce, pulling up, presently thrust out an arm, determinedly waving them more to the left. "I dunno about you," he said in Parras' direction, "but I've had all I want of this clawin'. If that joker with the saddlegun is still keepin' tabs he'll be up in them rimrocks. Mebbe we can flush him."

This suited Parras. These boys hadn't been near enough to see the burned hooves of that cow he'd put his rope on or to have caught the exchange between Wells and himself. Although it did not seem likely, there was always the chance the jigger who had been so free with that rifle was also the one who had burned that cow's toes. Parras was a long way from taking the blame off Indigo but if someone else was discovered in these parts he'd feel a mite more willing to consider himself mistaken.

As they pushed their horses up out of the bottoms the terrain grew steeper and considerably more open. Dappled with outcrops, this was not the best ground to be caught on if more blue whistlers were being readied to sail. The light was deteriorating with alarming rapidity, thickening up mighty soon to full dark.

Parras said, "How far you reckon we are from that wagon?" and the freckled hand answered, "Two miles mebbe. Lot shorter this way than if we'd gone the way Wells took. Here — git up there, dang you!" he yelled as one of their charges attempted to cut back.

Parras cuffed his hat at the steer, which shied back snorting in the wake of the others. When they rimmed out at the top the way grew even more open in a kind of long bench and once again Deuce pointed. "There's the fire. I could eat a goddam mule!"

If the pinpoint of winkery light the round-shouldered Deuce had his scrinched eyes fixed on was the Roman Four camp and cook's wagon they still had a pretty fair piece to go. In another ten minutes night would be all around them, hemming them in like the folds of a blanket, and this bench dropped off rather sharply just ahead into what appeared to be another wide slash of thorny brush.

But the freckled hand shook his head when Parras pointed this out. "Just low ground," he said, "filled up with shadders. Cholla and pear mostly — no place for that jasper to hole up down there."

Parras reserved judgment. These hands could be straight or up to their necks in this, ready to ride him smack into that gun. Nothing since he'd quit that dead horse at the bottom of Tenkiller appeared to be quite what it seemed on the surface. Paid a man in this country to stay on his toes and, dropping back a little to get out of the lead, Parras lifted the Winchester from under his strirup and rode with it cradled across his lap.

If the pair ahead noticed they kept their jaws out of this. Where the trail opened up enough to make this practical they swung out right and left to flank the pushed dogies, leaving Parras to ride the dust of the drag.

This indifference only served to tighten Parras' vigilance. His eyes were never still, grimly picking and prying at the roundabout shadows with the look of a man expecting Indians to jump him. He wasn't sure why he felt so keyed up unless it was the memory of that slug whipping past him.

When they dropped off the bench into the heavier dark of the cactus-studded flats it was Parras, still jumpy, who discerned the first hint of unidentified movement. Deeper into the black of these piled-up shadows he glimpsed a stirring like smoke stringing past on an air current, a tagend of motion quickly swallowed in the gloom. "On the left — watch it, fellers!" he sang out, lifting the rifle.

The nearest man, Deuce, twisted around in his saddle, palming his six-shooter but not finding anything to pin his sights on. As he hung there undecided a flutter of hooves barreling into the east jerked him up in his stirrups. Deuce caught at Parras' hand as he flung up the rifle.

"Wait — " Deuce growled, peering after the hoof sound. "About the only thing shootin' 'round here is like t' git us is a stampeded herd. That was cattle, not riders. You an' Nevada take after 'em; I'll stay with these critters."

The freckled hand put his mount into a lope. Parras kicked his horse after him and, not at all reassured, kept hold of his Winchester. They pushed into the felt-thick folds of the night side by side, running freely till Nevada, slowly, pulled Parras to a walk. "Hold on," he grumbled and, with their horses stopped, both men sat listening.

There was no sound of hooves, nothing to be heard except an updraft of wind and on this a faint throb of singing coming up from the south where the boys riding night herd were circling the cows.

"Reckon we've lost 'em?"

"Maybe they've cut back," Parras said, and kneed his mount into the north a couple rope-lengths, still gripping the rifle, eyes searching the gloom between stands of cholla, slowly walking the horse, Nevada beside him standing in his ox bows, head canted like a listening owl's.

"Over there," he growled, abruptly rigid, facing into the west. "Shake out your rope — try to get 'em between us." He kicked the steel into his horse and tore off, loop swinging, moving west, slightly south, at a hard driving run.

48

Parras, not convinced and filled with suspicions, struck out to the north of him still gripping the Winchester, reluctant to sheathe it lest these alleged cows turn out to be powder-burners. Be a fine kettle of fish if, put on notice, he walked right into it.

Had the girl set him up for this?

He didn't want to think so. Seemed a heap more likely if anything developed it was born of whatever lay between this spread and the Romero mayordomo. If there'd been trouble with Fay over previous counts, the Roman Four owner and his cow boss might have thought to see in Parras someone easier to bend if enough weight was leaned on him.

It made a kind of sense. Seen in this light that slug winging past could have been a sort of warning, combining threat and promise of what a man could look for if he took his job too serious.

It could also, of course, have been meant flat out to kill him.

He found himself wondering what the girl was really like behind the fright and fits of arrogance — not that he had much time to thing about this.

A cow bawled ahead of him and he used his spurs, driving alongside half a dozen critters, hollering, flapping his hat at the nearest, endeavoring to swing them south where Nevada, coming up, could turn them into a mill. He had to lean way out and cuff the felt hard against that bony head before the stubborn beast shied off, taking the rest of them lumbering with her into a wheel that turned on itself as Nevada dived at them swinging his rope.

Parras let go some of his held breath when the animals eventually milled to a stop. He sloshed the hat on his head but kept tight hold of the rifle as Nevada drifted over, sleeving sweat from freckled cheeks.

"We worked these flats movin' south two days ago," he said, sounding puzzled. "How you reckon this bunch got missed?"

Parras said, "Let's have a look at them. Powerful puny seems like, most of 'em, for full-grown critters — muleys, at that. Strike a light."

The freckled hand hesitated. "I'd sure hate to put them herds in a run . . . "

"Cup it in your hands."

Nevada sat very still, probably having a look at the Romero rep's rifle, which stuck out across Parras' legs in a no-nonsense fashion that must have been disconcerting.

He sighed in the panting silence like a wore-out horse. "So they're calves," he grumbled, "all but that one. Can't we just as well look at them back at the wagon? We don't git there mighty soon cook'll throw it away."

"Strike a light!"

Nevada, getting a match from his hatband, scratched it across the brass horn of his saddle.

Parras said, "Move around. I figure to see all of them. Particular the brands."

The five calves were marked with a IV. The cow, obviously fresh, was branded Two-Pole Pumpkin.

CHAPTER
EIGHT

A couple of the calves shifted restively, bawling. As the match burned down, one of these, lunging, ducked past two others to come against the cow where, with noisy satisfaction, it began to suck.

Parras, finger through trigger guard, waited for Nevada to exercise his talking talents.

The Madigan hand didn't appear in any hurry to burst into speech.

Any man familiar with the habits of cattle would have to be aware that mother cows and their calves, should they happen to get separated, would backtrack for miles to reach the spot at which each lost sight of the other. Neither man could doubt this was what had happened here.

Parras did not have to examine the cow to be reasonably certain she'd been hot-footed like that other one he'd looked at with Indigo Wells. Though unable to make out the Madigan hand's expression through the dark closing in upon that dropped match, Parras coldly watched for sign of hostile intent.

Nevada, still unmoving, finally said with an obvious reluctance, "Expect we better push this bunch back to camp . . . " kind of letting it hang there like he'd run out of wind.

Parras said: "I'll be interested to hear how this stacks up to your way of thinking."

"Some son of a bitch has been plenty busy. Yorba ain't goin' to like this a little bit — "

"That makes two of us," Parras said dryly.

There wasn't much use trying to locate Deuce; he was probably long since back at the holding ground with the steers they'd jumped up out of that brush. Waving the freckled man ahead of him Parras growled, "Get 'em started," and fell in behind as Nevada, grumbling, shook out his rope.

When they came in sight of the Roman Four camp — moved since they'd left in mid-afternoon — the crew, except for the four riding circle, were gathered at the wagon, most of them sprawled around the fire. "Get Yorb over here," Parras said gruffly, halting their gather well away from the herds.

Nevada let out a hail and while they were waiting Parras put away his Winchester, not neglecting, however, to keep an eye on his companion. The calf went back to nuzzling its mother.

Yorba, limned against the fire, strode phlegmatically toward them.

Parras, stone faced with both feet in the stirrups, said as he came up, "Nevada being one of your own, this'll be easier to take, I reckon, coming from him," and nodded at the hand who, without beating around any bushes, put Yorba in the picture.

Deuce drifted up as Nevada was unloading the unwelcome facts.

52

The cow boss looked the animals over, several times twisting unreadable glances at Nevada, who looked about as comfortable as a tenderfoot trapper who had just skinned a skunk.

Parras kept his mouth shut and waited.

Shouting for Wells and appearing meaner by the minute Yorba scowled at the calf where it stood spraddle-legged with its head tucked under the Two-Pole Pumpkin cow.

The freckled puncher said anxiously, "About three-quarters of an hour before we jumped these critters somebody took a shot at this feller."

Yorba, nodding, threw an irritable look at where Wells was disentangling himself from his eating tools. Without much evidence of interest he said, "Yeah. Deuce already told me." With his glance sliding around he asked in Parras' direction: "What you figure we ought to do about this?" indicating the animals with the lift of an arm.

"Reckon that's rightly up to you."

Yorba said testily, "I know who it's up to. You're here on behalf of the Romeros. This," he growled, stabbing a finger at the nursing calf, "belongs to that cow — not much doubt about that. What settlement you reckon will suit Olivares?"

"I expect the Romeros will probably want to know who them other calves belong to."

Indigo Wells came up while the cow boss was staring. "You figurin' to suggest them calves might not be ours?"

"Not my function. You asked for an opinion. I gave it."

Indigo, bristly as a bucketful of cholla, said: "Considerin' that critter me an' you jumped up before you went off to find this varmint I'd say you ain't got a heap of room to talk!"

Deuce stepped back. Nevada's mouth hung open.

Ignoring the hand Wells had wrapped about his pistol Parras said to Yorba, "It's your decision. You go ahead and settle this any way you want."

The cow boss' half-shut eyes held the shine of calculation. "All right," he mouthed smooth as peeled poles, "we'll let it go like it lays. You can vent that calf and we'll consider the matter settled."

Catching hold of Indigo's arm Yorba walked him off in the direction of the fire.

Parras shook his head at the freckled hand's offer to help with the venting. He wasn't taking Yorba's say-so on anything, certainly not on something as potentially explosive as tampering with the brand that had been run on that calf. He drove it with its mother into the herd being held for absent owners, leaving Nevada to dispose of the other calves. They might belong to Roman Four but could just as easily belong to someone else, forceably separated from their mothers.

Nothing was settled to his way of thinking. Yorba might choose to sweep this under the rug, but with all the witnesses working for Madigan he might find it convenient — if the cards shaped up right — to make Parras the goat and shut his mouth with a bullet. It wouldn't be the first time a feller plumb innocent was left to rot beneath a rustler's epitaph.

The possibility was not so far-fetched as he would like to have felt. They could pull some cutbank down over him and forget the whole thing if it suited their book, simply letting it be known he had rolled up his twine and gone to look for greener pastures.

Who would tell it different?

It had been for some contingency of this sort, no doubt, that Yorba had decided to separate the reps, never coupling two of them in any chore likely to take them out of sight. If it came right down to it, the way things stood now, they could spin any yarn that suited them about this.

It put a prickly feeling along his damp spine.

As Nevada had said, some son of a bitch had been plenty busy.

Regardless of whether Roman Four was back of this the freckled hand would likely string along with whatever story Yorba chose to give out. And if he wasn't that loyal he would see quick enough where he would he left on any other basis.

Teresa, Parras remembered, had made it pointedly plain there'd been trouble before on previous cow hunts between Fay and Yorba over the count; and Don Adolfo, when she had suggested they send Parras to Roman Four, had seemed to get pretty excited about this, appearing to favor Olivares' use of Joel Fay, the red-necked half gringo yank-and-shoot artist. "Olivares," the old man had wheezed, "understands what makes these Texicans tick."

But he hadn't sent Olivares. And Olivares, apparently, hadn't sent Fay . . . or had he?

Parras, headed for the fire in the hope of talking coosie into warming something over, found himself rather gingerly wondering if it was Fay, lurking out of sight somewhere in the brush, who had chucked that slug at him.

CHAPTER
NINE

Joel Fay had indeed been the one who had sent that slug on its way. In such cold turkey fashion he was not in the habit of watching the target continue to breathe, much less be in shape to ride off out of range, forewarned and therefore infinitely more dangerous to deal with in future; and he damned Parras roundly.

He was upset almost to the point of hysteria to have had this drifter in his sights and not drop him. The son of a bitch must have moved! It was the only answer Fay could come up with that left room for pride and his gunfighter's vanity. The wind might have shifted or dropped as he fired but that chance had been weighed with considerable care. He could not believe his aim had been faulty.

Though he could not acknowledge any error in self the corrosive glimpse he'd caught of Parras departing built a cold slime of sweat at the grip of his hatband and left him shaking in a frenzy of anguish. In Fay's line of business no taint was attached to shooting from ambush; this was one of the advantages employed by his kind. The inexcusable concept was to have had such an edge and see the fellow ride off. He could not envisage a blunder, could only curse and grind his teeth in the outrageous evidence of this hated man's luck.

There was something about this Johnny-come-lately that made a man squirm just to think about bracing him. Forewarned was forearmed . . .

True, he'd handled Parras once when the man was exhausted, scarcely half an inch from pooped after staggering through them damn thorns all the way from Tenkiller in that mid-morning heat with the sun bright enough to pretty near put your eyes out. Yet even then — now Fay came to think back on it — there'd been something unsettling about that big bastard.

Fay tried to pin down what it was had been gnawing him but all he could come up with was the look of those eyes . . . about as hard a pair as he had ever peered into. And now, with all his muscles jerking, he had to some way shore up his resources toward making another try. In his present unsettled state he couldn't think which was worse, facing Parras or going back to Olivares with a confession of failure.

It was not a choice at all inclined to ease the cramps he felt knotting his belly.

Back at the Roman Four wagon there was something cramped too in the stance of the horsey-faced owner as, pawing his jowls with an irascible hand, Madigan surveyed his lumpy-cheeked range boss. "Jesus Christ," he exclaimed in a passion, "with all the help you had standin' around why for Chrissake didn't you plant him right then?"

Though he darkened up some Yorba made visible effort to hang onto his cool. "I didn't plant him right then because there's too goddam much to this deal I don't savvy."

With their eyes still locked the range boss said, "He may be just a tough hand dug up to replace Fay or he could be a John Law drifted in from the U. S. Marshal's office with enough up his sleeve to tuck us away for a considerable while longer than I want any part of.

"Until I know where we stand I figure that play was the cheapest way out of this. If you want Wells turned loose you better climb on a horse and ride out there and say so. No mistake of that kind's goin' to be chalked up to me."

Madigan's long horsey face with its scraggle of whiskers tightened up around a temper that looked about to get away from him. "Maybe," he said, "you better start remembering who pays your wages . . . "

"I ain't never been left in any doubt of that," Yorba drawled with his bold and lively features strengthening the ambiguity of the shifted glance he laid on the other. "Long as I take your money I'll do what I consider to be in your best interests. Whether it suits your notions or not."

That was pretty strong talk and after pushing it around through his head for a moment Madigan backed off. "What is it about this you don't savvy?"

"I don't know, for one thing, who sent him out here. You had a note from the girl, but it's your friend Olivares who's been running that outfit. Since when has that girl been giving any orders? Was it her father put her up to this?"

When Madigan, apparently, had no ready answers, Yorba in that probing tone asked, "If the girl sent him over without Olivares' knowledge why hasn't that Mex hung Fay around our necks like usual? You suppose this jigger could of put Fay out of action — or Olivares mebbe? That could account for her gettin' into this . . . It all shakes down to who is this duck and what purpose he figures to serve showin' up here."

"We should of fixed up a accident for Fay last spring."

"Sure," Yorba sneered, "and had Olivares shoutin' to high heaven we been stealin' Romero blind. Ain't no way in the world with Joel Fay stomped on you could tie that slippery son — "

"There ain't nothing in my book," Madigan snarled, "which says that Olivares bears a charmed life!"

"You got a mighty short memory if you don't recollect the threat he laid on us of what's like to happen if somethin' stops his clock."

"I don't think he ever wrote no letter!"

"You can believe what you like. It ain't goin' to help if a letter turns up."

Madigan said grumpily, "How much rope you going to give this Parras?"

"Not an inch more'n I have to. He's bein' watched, you bet. Sooner or later him — or someone else mebbe — is gonna tip his hand . . . "

"And what do you reckon will happen if the son of a bitch gets next to this deal or finds out what poor

60

breeders them Two-Pole Pumpkins have stacked up to be?"

"I don't believe," Yorba said, "in crossin' bridges till I see 'em. And if I see anything like that shapin' up I'll bury the bastard so deep, by Gawd, time the light ever hits him they'll think he's the goddam missin' link!"

Olivares, after sending Fay off to block any chance of a confrontation arising from Parras' presence at the cow hunt, still could not altogether rid his mind of the creeping unease occasioned by the girl's unexpected interference coming so sharply on the heels of this new man's advent.

His disquiet, of course, went deeper than that, had a lot more substance, much more to feed on: a combination of features which, appearing to coalesce, must have rattled a man less firmly entrenched.

Recognition had been instant, a full awareness churning through Olivares the moment he'd clapped eyes on the man at the crossroads hamlet of Hatch four nights ago.

Though it had not then occurred to Polito to hook Parras up with Sig MacGurdy, the Socorro banker, it had given him a considerable turn to discover that hardnose prowling this close to home. So disturbed had the mayordomo been he'd hung around for a while, staying back out of sight, curious to learn what sort of inducement could have fetched a gringo of Parras' caliber into an area so unlikely as Hatch.

When the man had got onto his horse and set off Olivares piled into the saddle himself, nervous, almost jumpy in the rush of wild thoughts wheeling through his head. He had not suspected when he took up the trail the gringo would head like a homing pigeon for the same jag of country the mayordomo had settled on.

By the time he was certain Parras meant to skirt Tenkiller the Romero ramrod had worked himself into a considerable sweat. Till then there had been at least the chance the man meant to swing upcountry or maybe head south. Beyond Tenkiller, though, there was only one outfit in front of his tracks that Parras would conceivably head for this late.

Two-Pole Pumpkin.

Olivares shivered. It was like a cold breath had curled around his neck.

He had sat a moment, indecisive, finally grunted, having made up his mind. Knowing this country like the palm of his hand he'd slid from his mount and, lugging his rifle, struck off at an angle through the thorny scrub growth, swinging back to the trail where it came looping up through house-size boulders to lead sharply east along the brink of the cliff.

It was dark with the stars jumbled high overhead, but not too dark to hear the scuffling approach of the horse bearing Parras coming out of those rocks . . .

Even now Olivares, thinking back through the hours, could hear in his mind the clink of those shoes striking sharp against rock, but he put this away from him, wondering again as so often before how much he might lean on Parras' alleged loss of memory.

Sweeping a final shrouded look across the fortlike house with its tacked-on veranda he turned angrily away to rope out a horse. It was time in his head to pay MacGurdy a visit.

CHAPTER
TEN

Parras, searching the scrub next morning with the round-shouldered Deuce and Indigo Wells, uncomfortably wondered if he wasn't maybe being seven kinds of fools staying on with this outfit. In the trend things were taking he had his neck stuck way out. He might not remember what had fetched him to this country but he needed no crystal ball to be aware of the unremitting scrutiny Yorba's hands were laying on him.

A man would have to be a complete jackass not to sense the violence building up in this vicinity. Whether Madigan and/or his burly range boss were mixed up in this business one thing by now appeared amply apparent: *somebody* was certainly tampering with Romero's natural increase. No tally was needed after what he had seen to prove the old man's calf crop would have to be sold by book count if Two-Pole Pumpkin was to show any profit.

It was one thing telling himself this was no skin off *his* nose but something else trying to tell this bunch he was not here hunting stones to turn over. Man could talk himself plumb blue in the face. And, come right down to it, he was far from convinced — even if left to his own devices — that he would be content to let this deal run its course. Conscience a man might be able to ignore but the pull of that girl was like a new wine.

She was in his thoughts too strong and too frequent and he could finger few things more foolish than that. Until he learned who he was and what he was here for any truck with a woman looked too much like a death warrant.

What he ought to do, plainly, was ride back to Romero's, report what he'd seen and shake the dust of this country before that bird with the rifle got lucky. Nobody was like to miss him three times running.

"Running!" he grunted, and took another look at the things in his head. Something about the notion of flight felt a heap too familiar. Like a trail worn into ground too much traveled. He could feel the sweat cracking through his pores. Had he come into these hills to get *away* from something? Was it the reflection of some long ingrained habit that put this sudden unease churning through him?

Again he tried to rip the veil aside, sensing an urgency he could not define behind this shroud that was blanketing his past. What had he been before that fall from Tenkiller? What was he doing in country that held no recognizable features? Was he, in fact, some kind of damn fugitive running blind out of fright from some unbearable consequence?

The string-thin Wells with his pinched feral stare said sarcastically, "Well! You goin' to or ain't you?" with a thin held patience.

Parras, thus rudely jolted back to the realities, hauled in a long breath and grumbled, "Sorry. Expect you better ride that trail again."

"Somethin' on your mind you want I should make allowance for?"

Parras gave him back that inscrutable stare. "Been trying to think how I come to be here . . . where the hell I was going when I went over that cliff."

"Cliff?"

"Tenkiller."

"You went over Tenkiller?" The Roman Four gun hand looked his disbelief. "What kinda crap is that?"

The truth, Parras reckoned, appeared as good a bet as any. He said, shaking his head, "I woke up five days ago at the bottom of that drop alongside a dead bronc. Around noon I stumbled into the yard at Romero's, slept the clock around and was asked by the girl to make a hand at your cow hunt. Before that drop I could of been the Queen of Sheba for all I'm able to recollect now."

Deuce stared open mouthed. Wells looked skeptical. Parras, hauling his hat off, said, "Put your hand on my head if you figure I'm lyin'."

Wells said, "Deuce, go feel of this hombre," and dropped a hand beside the butt of his pistol, backing his horse to get out of Deuce's way.

The round-shouldered puncher, reaching out from his saddle, rather gingerly obliged. "He's got a scab there, all right, an' a lump big enough to take a hitch around. Ain't it sore?" he said to Parras.

"Well, I know it's there. Which is more'n I could say if it had been my neck."

Wells with a noncommittal shrug said dryly, "A gun barrel coulda put that on you."

"Maybe you'd like to ride over that way and have a look at the horse?"

"I don't think so," Wells said. "If this is somethin' you've fixed up I expect — "

"Now why would I do that?"

"It don't make no never-mind to me," Wells grunted. "My job right now is to round up cattle and the sooner we git busy the sooner we'll be done." He made an irritable shift of his weight in the saddle and to Deuce he said, hard eyes still on Parras: "You stick with him, Deucey, case he happens to wander off an' forgets whereabouts is the wagon."

As they lounged around the fire that night after chuck Madigan, the Roman Four owner, stepped through the clutter of gear and hands to stop beside Parras where he sat with his back propped against a shielding rock.

"Understand you've lost your memory, Parras."

"You have a look at that horse?"

"Yorba did."

"It tell him anything?"

"Buzzards been at it. Between them and the coyotes there wasn't much left. Do you remember the brand?"

"I took particular notice: Bar Six."

"Made how?"

Parras showed him with the bar on top.

"No brand like that around here."

"Figures." Parras nodded. "Or someone would of made me out before now. Hell, I'm not even sure Parras is my monicker — I been goin' by these," he said, digging out the papers he had shown Teresa and later retrieved from under Joel Fay's horse.

Madigan, squinting, held them up to the light. "Humph," he grumbled. "No brand mentioned."

"Yeah . . . does seem kind of odd, now you mention it." Putting them carefully back in his pocket Parras allowed it was his intention, once they were through here, to *pasear* up to the countyseat and have a look through the books.

Madigan grunted. "Ain't got but three local brands and the ones to each side of us." He rasped his jaw with the heel of a hand. He said, shifting weight, "You never come from around here." And a fretting scowl dug its tracks around his mouth. "Seems like you'd be curious what fetched you over here."

"It'll come to me, probably, one of these days. Like," Parras said, "howcome I'm packing two hundred bucks worth of foldin' money."

The eyes in Madigan's horsey face narrowed then scrinched as though puzzled. "Sounds like a walkin' temptation," he grumbled. "Was I you I'd sure not want that bunch you're shacked up with breathin' down my neck."

With a final hard look he took off toward the wagon. But horse sound, coming up from the south, spun him around like the yank of a rope to stand stiffly peering into the dark. Yorba, beyond him, slipped away from the

68

fire and Indigo Wells, letting go of a coffee mug, faded from sight off back of the wagon.

Parras kept to his seat, both arms crossed on kneecaps as he took all this in through the loudening clamor of the oncoming hooves. He watched the rider come plunging up out of the murk and guessed before the horse was pulled up on the sliding haunches this was going to be someone from Two-Pole Pumpkin.

He had Fay in his head and now was surprised to discover the rider was Teresa Romero.

CHAPTER
ELEVEN

She was windblown and flushed from the stares leveled at her, yet pride was in the hard turn of her chin and the sweep of her glance crossing Parras' face went headlong slamming into Madigan's scowl. "Where's Fay?" she cried through the drift of dust as if suspecting he'd been hidden purposely to spite her.

It got peculiarly quiet save for what scraps of breeze limped in off the desert to flap coosie's tarp and tug here and there at neckerchiefs and vest flaps. The Roman Four owner finally dragged off his hat, impelled by a grudging civility he made no effort to conceal. "There ain't no Fay in my paybook," he rumbled, tacking on testily, "If it's that sawed-off lead-chucker we've had so much guff from on other cow hunts you're augerin' about he ain't been around here. And there'll be no tears shed if he never is again."

The girl's angry eyes jumped to Parras bright with panic and, abruptly, disbelieving, stabbed at Madigan again. "Olivares sent him over here!"

Madigan slanched a look across his crew. "Any of you saddle-warmers seen the little scorpion?"

When no one spoke up he turned back to Teresa. "That satisfy you, missy?"

The girl didn't say but appeared in the interim to have got some kind of grip on herself and now, to Parras, she crisply bade, "Go catch up your horse."

Madigan exploded. "Now you look here, missy! You pull that waddie off the job don't expect *me* to look out for your stuff — we got all we can tend to lookin' after our own!"

Her scornful stare eyed him up and down. "I wouldn't worry about that. If Olivares sent Fay over here he'll *be* here."

Parras, pushing to his feet, took the rope off his saddle and struck out to get his mount while Madigan, stung, sent up a great shout. "If that son of a bitch comes sidlin' around I won't be responsible for what happens to him!"

"Whenever was a Texican responsible for anything?" She smiled at him thinly. "I expect Joel Fay can look out for himself."

She ignored their hard glances with the assurance of a *rico* and when Parras got back with his horse in tow she sat coolly waiting while he made ready to ride. When he swung up into the saddle Madigan said, dark-faced, in a hate filled voice: "You can tell your old man an' that connivin' Olivares the next Pumpkin rider caught on my range'll wish by Gawd he had never been borned!"

Teresa reined her horse about and Parras followed her away from the camp through a silence bristling with unconcealed hostilities.

He didn't break into her thoughts for some while, being content to pick over his own speculations, sorting out the impressions her presence had inspired, weighing his conjectures in the light of what he'd heard. But natural curiosity prompted him to ask, "What's with Fay to get you into such a lather?"

She didn't seem straight off to be inclined to answer. They rode perhaps another quarter mile before she turned to him abruptly. "My father has disappeared."

Parras peered at her, astonished. He said, trying to grasp the possibilities implied, "I had the idee he was a prisoner, a kind of hostage for your compliance . . . "

"He was — we both were," she said grimly. "But he's gone, all right. Olivares has turned the place inside out. The whole crew's hunting; but Olivares is so devious I don't know what to think, really."

"You mean your father might not have left of his own volition?"

"I don't honestly see how he *could* have. They've been watching us like hawks. Day and night Olivares has had us under constant — I mean even in our rooms we've not been free of this surveillance! Always there's been someone, generally two of them, keeping tabs."

Parras, thinking to reassure her, said, "But you got away."

She made a scornful sound but it was thick with despair. "I got away because the whole crew was gone, Olivares with them."

"If they've all gone I'd say he really must have escaped somehow . . . "

"You don't know Olivares, Parras! He's a master of deceit, believe me. He doesn't do things by halves. When he sets up something he goes the whole way. I'm afraid he's decided he can get along without us . . . or something may have forced his hand, made it imperative he shut Papa's mouth."

Parras stared his perplexity. In considerable anguish, she said, "After I sent you over here Olivares came back, furious to discover you were no longer there. I'm sure he guessed I had something to do with it. He sent Fay off — to this cow hunt, I thought — and right after that he went away, too, gone all the next day."

They peered at each other. Parras sighed. "I guess you know you're being stole blind . . . "

She waved that away, the measure perhaps of her preoccupation or the depth of her very real concern for her father. "I've never seen him so cold-faced mean. Most of the time he's got this toothy grin, like he's wondering which part of you to save for dessert. This morning he came storming into my room demanding to be told where Don Adolfo had got to. It was the first I'd heard . . . but you could tell from his eyes he meant it. They turned the place upside down, room by room, even tearing the peons' huts apart. He got an Indian in then looking for sign but of course by that time . . . Just short of noon they all rode away."

"And you still believe the whole thing was put on?"

"How could Papa have gotten out of there? I've tried myself any number of times — and why didn't he fetch that Indian at once? He's too shrewd to overlook anything so obvious. I didn't think of it then but if Don Adolfo had really escaped tracks would have been the first thing they looked for!"

"I don't know," Parras said. "In the shock of finding his hole card gone . . . " Too mixed up, he pawed at his face. "I still can't figure how Joel Fay's being at that Roman Four cow hunt — "

"But that's just it! I've no way of telling how long Papa's been gone! If Fay had been here we could have put more hope — at least there would still have been an outside chance Papa really . . . Don't you *see?*"

"Afraid that fall must've sprung — "

She didn't wait for him to finish. "Fay — when Olivares sent him off on that horse — may have gone somewhere else or simply scouted Madigan's camp and gone back with his report. We can't know what it was but something has certainly upset Olivares. If you'd seen his eyes when he came into my room!"

"If your father got away from him . . . "

"I can't believe that. He's been too befuddled, too drunk to outwit them."

Looking into those anxious eyes Parras asked, "What do you honestly reckon has happened?"

"They've taken him someplace else; I'm sure of it. Don't ask me why but I am terribly afraid that's where Fay has got to."

*Some*one would have to keep an eye on him, Parras reckoned. He could understand her getting the wind up if she really believed her father had been taken off against his will. But this didn't necessarily mean he'd been harmed. "If you're right in thinking he's been forcibly moved it was probably to put more pressure on you, a means of making you amenable to whatever it is Olivares has in mind. At a guess I would think he might

74

be beefing up his chances of talking you into double harness."

She seemed to consider, finally bobbing her head. "You may be right. In any event we must find my father. If they were to get away with something like that Olivares would have precisely what he's after, a hold on the ranch that nothing could shake. It would be just like putting a gun to Papa's head."

Parras stared uncomfortably. "Hard to imagine they would go that far . . . "

"It's not hard for *me!* You don't know them. Fay's a rattleweed smoker — he wouldn't stop to think twice. He'll do whatever Olivares tells him to."

"Well . . . " Parras shrugged. "Before you jump straight out of your skin let's get back to your place and take a look for ourselves. Smartest place for Olivares to hide him would be right on your spread where he'd have him handy."

CHAPTER
TWELVE

After the girl and Parras rode away from his camp Madigan, still seething, beckoned his cow boss aside. "You got any notion what all that was about?"

"Who could figure a woman?" Yorba curled back his lip. "You want my notion we're well rid of that jasper."

"By Gawd, I don't like it! She damn well had to be up to something sending a stranger over here in the first place. Now, before this hunt is half done with, she comes over herself and pulls him off. There's something sure as hell going on we ought to know about. Mebbe you better send one of the boys — "

"I ain't even sure he was workin' for her," Yorba growled, breaking in. "How do you know this goddam clown ain't somebody MacGurdy has saddled off on us?"

Madigan's scowl rimmed his mouth with deep creases. Yorba said, "Mebbe you should go have a talk with that banker."

Madigan, pushing it around, muttered, "Maybe I should, but that girl come in here like the tail of a twister and was twice as shook up when she didn't find Fay."

"Could be she's sweet on him."

Madigan snorted. "A guy like that she wouldn't give the time of day! Somethin' else I don't like is what she said about him — remember? — about Olivares sending him over here. How come he ain't showed?"

Yorba shrugged. "Mebbe this Parras has took care of the bugger. I — " Sucking his breath in the cow boss suddenly slapped a leg. "Christ! Mebbe it was *Fay* took that shot at Parras!"

Madigan, sharply considering, nodded. "But it still don't explain what's got into that girl. Something's happened back at their place for her to come tearing after Fay like that an' then, not finding him, takin' off with Parras. I say we better find out. Maybe you better look into it yourself."

Yorba held up a hand, bending forward, listening, smiling thinly as he straightened beefy shoulders. "I sent a boy over there to have a look around yesterday. Expect this is Petey comin' in now."

Madigan, too, had caught the shuffle of hooves and wheeled to throw a look in their direction, suddenly swearing. The grin slid off Yorba's face like melted grease. "Goddam!"

It was Fay who'd come into the light and now came off his saddle with a jingle of spur chains. With his mouth sullenly creased and wary eyes watchful he picked his way past the fire to come up on their flank as though rather gingerly looking for trouble and not too certain he'd be able to avoid it.

"You took long enough gittin' over here," grunted Yorba, and Madigan said, "Did you know your lady boss was hunting you?"

Fay's amber eyes in that sun-peeled face flicked from one to the other, uneasily endeavoring to focus on both. He passed a dry tongue across drier lips. Yorba's sneer, paraded with malevolence, suggested he would welcome any belligerence Fay might launch. "Cat's got his tongue," he railed, and laughed at the color driven into Fay's cheeks.

"What did she want?" Fay asked Madigan stiffly.

"Good question," the Roman Four owner conceded. "We was kinda hoping you'd be able to tell *us*."

"She don't have no time for him now she's got Parras," Yorba said into the aggravated silence.

The Romero hand, flushing, took a hitch around his temper. He was in poor shape at this camp to burn powder. He cleared his throat to tell Madigan gruffly all he knew about her errand was he'd seen her and the new man humping their horses in the direction of the river.

Yorba said, "How long you been away from your place?"

Fay's eyes narrowed around the anger that stared out of them.

Madigan, not quite ready for an open break at this point, tried to spread a little oil across the heave of troubled waters. "If anybody's got the real word on Parras it'll be Joel Fay. Never misses a trick. Ain't that right, Joey?"

It's surprising the people gross flattery will get to. Straightening — not quite preening but perceptibly pleased — Fay filled his chest up with air to say, "We figger he's someone MacGurdy's sent in." He was too full of his own importance to straightaway note the shortness of fuse this careless talk had uncovered.

When the stillness began to take hold of his nerve ends he took a shocked second look in the direction of Yorba to find himself eyeing the naked snout of a gun.

It was all he had time for.

The rush of words piled up back of his teeth had not got past the drop of his jaw when the crash of that pistol slammed a hole through the night.

It was three or four hours later before Teresa and Parras hauled up panting mounts to stare down upon the blackness of her father's ranch headquarters. In that cricket-riddled quiet a feeling of abandonment seemed to permeate the darkness around those huddled lumps of buildings.

No faintest gleam of light was anywhere apparent. The girl, bending forward, would have sent her horse toward the yard at once had Parras not reached out and taken grim hold of the animal's bridle.

"Let's not go flappin' our wings straightaway. If there's nobody there it'll keep a spell longer." He could sense the tumult of impatience that was in her. She tried to knock his arm away. "If you're afraid," she said hotly, "you can stay up here while — "

"It's not so much a case of bein' afraid as of wishin' I might have been after it's too late. For all we know that place is filled with watching steel-armed spiers just waitin' for someone to waltz into their web."

"Are you proposing to sit here all night?" she whipped back.

"Being anxious is one thing, foolish somethin' else. You stay put," he said flatly, "while I take a look around."

Not waiting for any argument Parras kneed his horse, catercornering to the left behind the rim of the ridge where it dropped in a spur toward the open ground below. Moving only where the shadows lay deepest and with a gun in his fist, he sent the horse angling forward at a circumspect walk, not at all liking this but determined not to trigger any ambush that might be laid for the unwary.

Pausing frequently to listen, he came onto the flat. He had a feeling of having been through all this before but, try as he would, could detect no sense of danger. Perhaps Teresa's father really had escaped Olivares; but he found this hard to credit. It seemed a heap more likely the old man's disappearance was something Olivares had deliberately set up to put more pressure on the girl.

He moved into the yard, every inch of him alert, and still nothing happened. No movement snagged his roving eye, no untoward sound came out of the dark. He swept the yard once again then loudly hailed, "Anyone home?" wholly ready to duck at the first sign of peril. Nothing but the sound of his own voice came back to him.

He called the girl down and when she joined him told her: "You take the house. I'll go through these outbuildings. Look under the beds and turn out the closets. Check in back of things where there's any space at all between them and the walls. He could be tied up and gagged — even rolled inside of a carpet. Now keep your wits about you. Whatever else he may be this feller ain't foolin'."

Her eyes came around with what he took to be annoyance. In that blue murk of starshine he observed the rebellious tilt of her chin. "If there's anything peculiar, anything at all, don't dig into it. Yell for me an' make all the noise God'll let you."

CHAPTER
THIRTEEN

Madigan, at the Roman Four wagon, struck down Yorba's arm as the gun went off, driving the bullet between Fay's legs, where it whanged off a rock in screaming ricochet.

The cow boss swore.

"Don't be a goddam fool!" Madigan snarled while Fay stood locked in his tracks by fright. "This son of a bitch'll be no help to us dead!"

Reaching fast across Yorba he snatched the still holstered pisol away from Fay's thigh and stepped back, smiling thinly at the man's frozen face. "He's got a lot of things he's just bustin' to tell us; ain't that right, Joey?"

The Romero hand shivered. He had to lick his lips twice to get enough wet to talk with and even then his rusty voice seemed unable to shape any sounds that made sense. Staring, aghast, he jerked his head in a nod.

Yorba said, disgusted, "You can put in your eye all you'll git outa him!"

"Oh, I don't know," Madigan drawled. "A feller that's been right bower to Olivares ought to have any number of things flappin' around through his skull that a man in my boots would be happy to know."

Still smiling, the horse-faced Roman Four owner got out the makings and one-handedly shook together a smoke; he hung it on his lip while he looked Fay over. "You can start," he suggested with a wave of Fay's shooter, "by tellin' us why Olivares figures Parras is working for MacGurdy."

Fay, eyeing the pistol, swallowed uncomfortably. It was plain he wished he were a thousand miles away.

"Well?" Madigan prompted.

After several false starts the Romero hand blurted: "Alls I know is Olivares is afraid of him."

"He thinks Parras is faking about that lost memory?"

"I dunno about that. The night he's supposed to've fell offa that cliff — Parras, I mean — Olivares was gone. The girl wanted to see him an' he was noplace around. He come in about two. I heard somethin' so I got up an' looked. He'd stopped, crossin' the yard after puttin' up his horse — head bent like he was listenin'. Had his boots in his hand when he went pussyfootin' through that patio gate."

"You figure he didn't want to be seen?"

"Alls I know is he was sure in a stew when he come back the next evenin' an' found Parras gone. He give the girl a goin' over, not that he got anythin' out of her. He was sure some graveled thinkin' she had sent Parras over here."

"So then he sent you along to take care of Parras."

Fay opened his mouth and shut it again. He squirmed around in his clothes when Madigan, sloe eyed, said, "That's how it was, ain't it? You did take that shot at him."

The man reluctantly nodded.

"Must've kept you humpin' keeping out of our way." Madigan whipped a match across the seat of his pants and puffed fire into his cigarette. "If your boss wanted him took off the roster how come you ain't put a slug through him yet? That's what he sent you over for, wasn't it?"

"Well . . . that an' other things," Fay said sullenly. "I was supposed to take Parras' place at this cow hunt."

"Accordin' to your tell," Yorba growled, "you been out there somewheres pussyfootin' around the last three, four days. It take you that long to work up to a killin'?"

Hate jumped into the scrinch of Fay's stare and a darkening anger boiled into his cheeks. "Twice your knotheads screwed me out of a shot! I damn near had that scissors-bill tonight but that fool girl come up just as I was fixin' — "

"I wouldn't hire you," Yorba sneered, "to wipe my ass!"

Madigan said quickly: "You must have some sort of notion why your boss is so anxious to get shucked of Parras."

Fay pawed at flushed cheeks. He scowled, ignoring Yorba. "I'd say he was scairt that bird would remember him."

"So you figure them two have crossed trails before." Madigan woolling it around, said, "It seems you've

84

decided Parras *did* go over Tenkiller, evidently with some kind of assist from your boss."

Cigarette waggling a corkscrew of smoke the Roman Four owner asked abruptly: "What do you suppose he would want to do that for? And how did Polito know this feller would be available?" And Yorba said, "You reckon he sent fer him?"

Fay looked like they had him all tangled up. A wind off the river fetched the ululating rumor of a fast traveling horse. Yorba, springing to life, slipped around the wagon's tailgate and three of the hands that had been hugging the fire rolled hurriedly away from it while another pair jumped to their feet reaching hipward.

The rider came pounding into the light and Yorba, reappearing, called: "Petey! What did you find out?"

The new arrival, still in the saddle, cried, "That *borracho* Mex has slipped his picket pin! Olivares has got the whole crew out huntin' him!"

Teresa tossed her head and, getting down off her horse, struck out for the veranda. Peering after her a moment, half minded to call her back, Parras, growling under his breath, sent his mount toward the stables.

Afoot, gun lifted, he shoved open the door, ready to jump at the first sign of trouble. But there was no one inside, not even a horse. Which struck him as odd because there'd been no mounts in the day pen either. Had Olivares in his anger pressed even the cook aboard a bronc?

There were a heap of thoughts whirling around his head but he did not let these distract his attention or obscure the plain need for vigilance. He kept the gun in his fist and went through every stall, even moving sacked feed and then climbing into the loft to scuff about in the knee-deep hay. *Unless he's buried*, he finally decided, *the old man's not in here.*

Outside he stared at the house's lighted windows then, chewing his lip, headed for the bunkhouse — not because he thought her father would be over there but because it was nearest and it was his nature to be thorough.

He lit a lamp inside and saw at once the place was empty. He poked around just the same, looking for sign and not finding anything to suggest the man had been there.

He tried the forge shack next and then stood a while peering toward the huddle of huts occupied by the peons. A door slammed back of him and he wheeled to find Teresa crossing the yard.

"No luck?"

She shook her head.

He said, looking again toward those boxlike adobes, "Reckon we ought to talk to those folks?"

She struck off without answering, Parras trailing. But it did no good. Nobody there had seen Don Adolfo.

Back at the house Parras said, "Let's take another look at his room," and followed her through the patio gate. It was wasted time and she said as much, bitterly. There was no sign of blood, no evidence of struggle.

86

"Looks like he got away after all," Parras said, but the girl wouldn't buy that.

"You don't know Olivares." She said to him grimly, "Wherever Papa is he's still a prisoner."

"And you think Fay's with him?"

"I'm sure of it."

CHAPTER
FOURTEEN

But Fay wasn't with him. Fay was still disarmed at Madigan's wagon across the river, staring in astonishment at the hand who'd just told them of Don Adolfo's escape.

Yorba, too, had his mouth open, staring, but the Roman Four owner appeared to be seeing things not in sight, and this preoccupied look coalesced in decision as he reached out to grip the cow boss' arm.

He pulled Yorba aside with his eyes counting noses and said to the questioning look on his face: "Opportunity's knocking. You heard what Pete said: Olivares has his whole crew out hunting!"

The sandy-haired cow boss appeared caught in events that were happening too fast, and then his puzzled look cleared and his bullypuss features showed a bold and livening interest. "You mean while they're gone we should take over the spread?"

"Why not?" The glitter of greed was in Madigan's stare. "We've got Romero's notes for more than ten thousand! He can't show half the stock he put up for collateral! And if he's skipped he'll be in damn poor straights to scrape up even the interest on the note that falls due day after tomorrow!" Madigan took hold of the man's arm again. "We'll be only protectin' what'll come to us anyhow."

He could see that his cow boss was turning it over. The man was plainly all for it, but the cautious streak Madigan had cursed more than once was in Yorba's head rather obviously projecting the possible dire penalties if somewhere this slipped up.

Madigan's long horsey face with its scraggle of whiskers shoved closer to urge: "It's the chance of a lifetime!" His fingers tightened like the grip of a vise. "An' you won't be forgot if we put this over."

Yorba licked at his lips. "But we'll need the full crew to hold that place against Olivares. We can't pull all the boys off this job . . . "

"To hell with this job — we're gambling for stakes that make these cows look like peanuts! Let the reps hold these critters . . . "

"There's somethin' else you're forgettin'. Regardless of anything else," Yorba muttered, "that note comin' due is made out to the bank."

"That's where I'm one up on you." Madigan grinned smugly. "I've already got that last note, endorsed over. We'll have to fight off Olivares — not much doubt about that; but what has he got? A bunch of damn Mexicans with no more guts than this Fay! They'll dig for the tules once we've knocked off a few — an' we'll have Fay with *us!*"

"Well . . . " Yorba's cat-clever eyes searched his face with distrust. "But what's in it fer me?"

"I said I'd take care of you." Madigan punched Yorba's shoulder. "What do you say to a full quarter interest?"

Back at Two-Pole Pumpkin Teresa, looking beat, exclaimed: "What do we do now? Twiddle our thumbs until he gets in touch with me?"

Parras' glance held the shine of compassion — not that he was about to let her discover this. No girl raised as she must have been would accept for an instant either charity or pity from any out-at-heels gringo, especially from one who didn't know his own name.

Though there was considerable here he could not seem to get hold of he had no trouble understanding her torment. With her world being turned upside down — all the things she'd been crudely threatened with, the indignities and terrors that lurked on every side — and convinced as she was her dad was still in the clutches of their unscrupulous range boss, every thought of her tomorrows must appear worse than hopeless.

If Olivares *did* have the old man under his thumb there wasn't much anyone could do till he got hold of them — unless, of course, Don Adolfo could be located. Parras wasn't quite ready to face up to this. He wasn't at all sure Olivares had the man. "I think," he said, "we ought to see MacGurdy."

Teresa stared. "Whatever for?"

"He's your banker, isn't he?"

"What's that got to do with it?"

Parras said, "He might have information concerning your father's intentions . . . "

"Intentions!" she flared. "He's been stupid with *vino* ever since that man came here!"

"That doesn't make sense — "

"It makes as much sense as traipsing off to Socorro. We've got to find him, I tell you!" Her eyes were like whips in the look they put on him. "I daren't think what unspeakable things are being done while you stand there bickering — and Papa perhaps not three miles from this place!"

If Olivares had him she could be right about this, Parras privately conceded. What the man obviously wanted was the ranch and he would not balk at torture to get some kind of conveyance, not if he had got impatient enough to yank the old man out of here.

It might be that snatching the owner of record right out from under Madigan's nose was the likeliest means Olivares could take to make sure he came loose of whatever he'd got into, including what was happening to Romero's cattle.

The girl stirred impatiently. "You *did* say the smartest place Olivares could hide him was right on this ranch."

Parras tiredly sighed. "Guess I did," he admitted, wishing again he could rip aside whatever was keeping the past hidden from him. He had the prickly feeling if he could know what had brought him to the foot of Tenkiller he might be well on the way to unraveling this mess. And that didn't seem to make much sense either.

Irritably he said, "Has this outfit got any range camps?"

"We've corrals and a shack in the Cristobals."

"How far is that?"

"The other side of the river — about four hours with fresh horses. We haven't used it in years."

"Thought Roman Four held the other side . . . "

"This place is above them. The range claimed by Madigan was all part of ours until Texicans took over the recorder's office . . . but this is no time to go into local politics."

Parras, over an odd sort of look, asked: "Where do we get fresh horses?"

"We'll have to use those we've got. They turned everything out before Olivares took off."

"Where'd you get that one?"

"He came back for a drink." She swung into the saddle with a flutter of skirts. "Don't you want to get started?"

"Look," he said. "You weren't really figuring to — "

"I'm not staying here if that's what you're getting at." She considered his scowl with a toss of the head. "How do you suppose you would find it without me?"

Parras, shrugging, thrust a boot in the stirrup. "Lead off," he grumbled, not so much at her as at the things he could grimly imagine happening if Olivares returned in a vengeful mood. That fellow looked capable of just about anything.

She led north at a canter, impatient and reckless till Parras irascibly said, "Won't get there quicker by running their hocks off."

Stiffly angry, she pulled her mount down to a shuffling walk.

At the end of the first hour Parras pulled up where starlight showed a ridge of low hills ahead of them. Teresa said sourly, "Now what's the matter?"

"Better rest them a bit."

She fidgeted impatiently while Parras sat scanning the country around them. She had a quirt on her wrist and kept whacking her skirt with it. "While you're observing the beauties of nature that miserable thief could be forcing my father to sign over the ranch!"

Parras nodded. "That's a risk we can't do anything about." He saw the look that flashed out of her eyes. "You Romeros don't think much of gringos, do you?"

She started to say something, clamped her mouth shut; probably, he thought, because she had need of him. "Anglos," he said, "have no corner on treachery. People are people and they haven't changed much in two thousand years. You find good and bad in all races, Teresa."

That fetched her chin up. "What were you running from when you went over Tenkiller?"

"I don't know," he said shortly and kneed his horse forward. "Lead out and don't run them or we'll both be afoot."

She swung east in grim silence. Parras became lost in the turn of his thoughts, which went down a long spiral of lonely apprehensions as he considered the father and the forces in league to usurp this girl's inheritance. He thought of Madigan and Yorba, attempting to fit himself into their boots, wondering if this unscrupulous pair had corrupted Olivares. Or was it the other way around?

Near daybreak they came into a bosque, a low wooded trough between rimming hills, and spent half an hour tunneling through a crisscross of branches to come out with full light on a view of the river steeply guarded by vermilion cliffs.

"We're not like to get across that," he growled.

Teresa, still sulking, never even looked around. Striking north again, paralleling the river's course, she presently murmured, "There's a ford up ahead."

They reached it just as the sun came above the gilded rims of the mountain chain that was sprawled along the stream's far side. "Fra Cristobals," she noted with the wave of an arm.

While not enormously rugged they did take up a lot of country, dropping off south into the Caballos and rising north of San Marcial into the higher reaches of the Magdalenas. Parras, eyeing their transportation, shook his head dubiously.

But these Romero horses didn't know the word *quit*.

Six hours from Two-Pole Pumpkin Teresa and the man who called himself Parras sat panting mounts. They looked down on a shallow bowl lush with the waving stems of green grass that came belly-high on the twenty-odd head of piebald cattle unconcernedly browsing in strungout fashion between the bottom of this slope and a distant series of cedarpost pens.

Parras tiredly blew out a sigh. The girl's lips tightened.

There was a squatty log cabin just beyond the pens but no sign of horses and no smoke trickling out of the fieldstone chimney. "Go ahead," Parras said. "We've come this far. Might as well prove it out."

The girl continued to sit immovably staring. Parras, muttering, sent his horse down the precipitous slope along the series of switchbanks someone had blasted from the face of this rock. He was further convinced by the way the cattle flung up their heads that no people had passed this way in some while. But he went doggedly on across that green sea to pass the corrals and pull up by the cabin, contemplating the quiet while he waited for the girl to come up beside him.

"Nobody home." He pointed to the undisturbed ground by the doorsill. "No one's been at this place in months."

Teresa's eyes stared stonily. But she could not entirely hide the frustration or the frantic thoughts flapping through her head. In the cold morning light he saw the tremble of her lips and, calling himself seven kinds of sucker, said, "Now think. We're not like to get a third whack at this business. Is there any other place inside your dad's holdings where a man could be hidden or figure to hide out with any chance of success?"

She didn't answer at once but kept turning it over, frowning while she dug through the memories the years had piled up. At last she said hesitantly, "There used to be a kind of trashy settlement back on the Animas about ten miles above the ranch — I remember going

95

there once as a child before Papa had the place cleaned out."

Parras scrubbed at stubbled cheeks. "Do you think you could find it — from here, I mean?"

Their eyes met and locked. "I could try." She sighed, and he could see this was something they were going to have to do. The biggest thing in its favor from his viewpoint was that Olivares, being relatively new in his job as segundo and with a crew even newer, might not know about the place, or if he did know may have forgotten it. For Parras still wasn't as convinced of Romero's abduction as Teresa appeared to be. To his way of thinking Olivares, without he was suddenly desperate, had considerable to lose and little to gain by forcibly removing the old man from his home.

CHAPTER
FIFTEEN

The horses looked about to play out for sure when Parras, some three hours and many stops later, thrust out a hand to say flatly: "Without there's some place almighty damn handy we can get some fresh mounts and a bait of grub we ain't goin' to make it."

The girl's red-rimmed stare skittered over his face with more than a suggestion of downright uneasiness. "There's Chloride," she said, "and Chise farther west . . . too far off I'm afraid to be of much help. The only place really near is Cuchillo . . . "

"How far?"

"Maybe three *kilómetros*."

"If I put on a hog-callin' voice would they hear me?"

"Parras, I beg of you, don't!" she cried sharply. "We'd be fools to attract notice — more foolish to go there! It's as rough a place as you'll find north of Lordsburg, the hangout of men with a price on their heads — no sheriff or marshal has been near there in months!"

He showed a sardonic grin. "Aren't you bustin' to see how us damn Yankees live?"

"Parras, I'm serious! Those vultures — "

"So am I," he growled, scowling. "Without fresh horses we ain't going noplace . . . unless you're hankerin' to get on shanks' mare and hoof it. Way my backbone is sagging right now — hell! It's neck meat or nothing."

She considered him darkly. "You don't have to do this."

When he waved that away she said like it came straight out of the heart, "You've got your own life to live. What happens to my father — "

But he chopped that off, too. "I've got my hand to keep in. *You're* not quitting while the old man's away and I can't see myself bein' shown up by a filly that wouldn't weigh a hundred pounds if she was soaking wet. Wherat's this place?"

She started to turn away, then said like she'd come to the end of her rope, "What's the use? I don't have the price of a bowl of beans let alone two meals and a couple of horses in a place where your throat could get cut for two bits . . . "

"Expect I can scrape up enough for both of us."

An edge of surprise briefly glimmered like doubt in the turn of dark eyes. Then, facing front, she reined her horse to the right and sent the stumbling gelding down a shale-littered slope, Parras following.

He had never known a woman quite like her, he thought, or at least could not remember one. Whether she knew it or not, she was fighting for her life. That was what it amounted to when you took into account the kind of rannies she was up against.

In the swirl of mixed thoughts he went over them again: Madigan, Yorba, Fay and Olivares. He couldn't help feeling the Romero ramrod was the one who most mattered. He was the one nearest Teresa . . . the one who'd had her father so completely under his thumb. Regardless of which had instigated the theft of Romero cattle — and it might of course be a pooling of interests — it was Olivares and his gunfighter who posed, because of their proximity, the gravest threat to this girl's uncertain future.

They came out of a wash and saw Cuchillo before them, a scatter of shacks put together of bits and pieces. It set along the stretch of a stream that had finally quit running to show gray clutters of barren rock between stagnant pools half filled with old cans and a litter of garbage. The most pretentious building, gray like the rest from the inroads of weather, had three mounts racked before it and a stale smell of beer curling from its open door.

"Wait here," Parras clipped, coming out of the saddle with a quick glance about that showed him no one at all. His spurs dragged sound from warped planks as he went past the door to reel on through the dimness till he came against the bar.

There was no back mirror but shapes at either side of him gradually resolved into gun-hung men, and a scrinch-eyed barkeep with a bald head square in front of him. The bald head said, "What'll it be, mac? Beer or bourbon?"

"Neither just now, thanks. I'd like two sacked lunches and a pair of fresh nags if you've anything with bottom."

A kind of silence settled. Then a Texas voice back of him drawled, "Sounds like you're in sort of a hurry."

"I'm sure not planning to linger none." Without turning his head, braced for trouble, Parras said, "I want *good* horses and I'm willin' to pay for them."

"I dunno where'll you'll get 'em," the barkeep growled. "Good horses come high in these parts, mac — real high."

With a wintry smile Parras murmured, "Figures." And before things could get any worse in this jackpot he shot out both arms in a swift lunging move that tugged at necks on either side and swept heads together in a resounding crack.

He sent both men slamming into the bar and spun while the bald head was reaching for his sawed-off, coming up with a pistol and the single word *"Don't!"*

The barkeep froze. The Texan at the table showed a suddenly tickled face. "She always back you up like that?"

Teresa said from the door, "Sometimes I shoot if I get wrought up enough."

The Texan put his hands on the table, palms flat against the wood. "Sack a lunch for them, Talbert." To the half stunned pair still propped up by the bar he said, "You heard the little lady, gents. Just so's she won't get the wrong slant here I'd count it as a favor if you stepped out of them shell belts. Obliged," he drawled as these plopped to the floor. "Kick them over there by His Nibs."

"Never mind," Parras said. "I can stomp my own snakes. What's your stake in this play, mister?"

The seated man turned one spread-fingered hand over on the table to show its empty palm. "Not rightly sure I got one, Jack."

He had shrewd little eyes the color of pulled taffy, a flat crowned hat with pinned-back brim. A much wrinkled canvas coat was buttoned across his chest; and pants the color of rust, bulgy tight at hip and thigh, were shoved into the tops of brush-scratched mule-eared Justins.

The gangrenous hat, the saddle leather hue of sun-scrinched features, almost everything about him had the hardnosed stamp of Texas. "Been kinda thinkin'." He smiled across those uncallused hands. "I got a pair of bangtails you just might take a shine to." He included Teresa in that disarming spread of lips. "Time we git back Talbert'll have your grub ready."

"We'll look," Parras decided, and the man got up. The girl stepped back away from the door, one hand still grimly in the pocket of her skirt while Parras followed him onto the porch. "How far away is this?"

Canvas Coat said, "Just a few doors," stepping into the street, "and you won't have to cough up an arm or a leg. What profit I get comes outa fast turnovers."

A lot of it no doubt did, Parras reckoned. As a concession to the nature of this tucked-away community he had holstered his six-shooter; but his stare roved the dusty road with the vigilance of a hawk while he kept one eye bleakly fixed on their guide, more than half suspecting they were being led into a trap.

They had not gone more than three or four rope lengths when Canvas Coat turned off toward a ramshackle barn set back perhaps a hundred yards in a clutter of broken-down machinery that looked to have been hauled from the shafts of abandoned mines.

It crossed Parras' mind to leave the girl outside but there were risks to that too. Trailing the man through the open door, eyes watchfully narrowed, he heard Teresa back of him picking her way around a tangle of baling wire. The barn had five stalls, three of them occupied by rangy looking geldings that nickered at their approach.

"These two here," their guide said, gesturing.

"You want to fetch out that bay and lead him around?"

The fellow picked up a halter and, slipping it over the bay's head, backed him out.

"Let's have a look at them feet," Parras said. The girl, hand in pocket, kept her mouth shut. She may have had a derringer there. Parras said to her, "Hold onto him," and, to Canvas Coat, "Now the other one."

There were brands on these animals, both of them different. "Any papers?" Parras asked.

The man grinned thinly. "For eighty-five dollars you gonna holler about papers?"

"Eighty-five for the pair?"

"Does it look like I got a hole in my head?"

Parras studied him briefly, in no position to insist on such niceties. "I'll take them," he said and pulled out his roll, peeling off the asked amount, putting what was left of it back in his pocket. "You got shanks for these halters?"

The man dug up two lengths of cotton rope, from which Parras fashioned a pair of workable bridles. "Climb aboard," he told the girl and, after mounting himself looked down at the man with a crusty stare. "After you," he murmured, following Canvas Coat out, pulling up in the yard until Teresa came alongside.

Eyes rummaging the street he looked both ways but, as before, it seemed devoid of life. One might have imagined that the denizens of Cuchillo were hell-bent on staying out of other folks' business but Parras had other notions on this subject. He was betting dollars against doughnuts it was the kind of place where all were aware of the tiniest ripple, probably crouching right now beside their hardware and bolt holes, waiting to see what would come of this intrusion. And the pressures holding them rooted for the moment would be doubly corrosive in that pair he had sent reeling into the bar.

From his placement in this yard the saloon wasn't visible, only a front edge of it showing, and the drooping shapes of the worn-out horses standing spraddle-legged before that peeled pole hitchrail.

To Canvas Coat Parras said, "If you're smart you'll leave well enough alone," and, nodding at Teresa, kneed his mount into motion, quitting the yard at a leisurely walk, pointing the sorrel to the bar through the dust of the road.

It had been a long time since he had forked a horse bareback and it astonished him considerably to discover he remembered this. He only hoped the girl could stick on that bay. After a moment, from the side of his mouth he said, "Catch yourself a good grip in his mane and be ready to stampede hard to the right when I give you the sign."

He didn't look at her. There were some things a man had to take on trust.

Parras didn't reckon he was done with this yet . . . not, leastways, in that Texican's notion. It was Canvas Coat who'd disarmed those boys. And if he could do this without lifting voice or even raising a finger why should he let this windfall elude him? On horses he could plainly sell time after time.

And if it hadn't been horses it would be something else. Had them all set up to go back for the grubsack, two sitting ducks already scheduled for planting. "*Now!*" he growled and, hauling his mount around, drove in the spurs.

Rifles banged back there by the saloon but distance and angle were scarcely conducive to spectacular gunnery. It was Canvas Coat a man had to watch out for and, true to form, the son of a bitch was taking chips, running into the road, naked shooter in his lifted fist.

There was no charity left in Parras. Whipping out his pistol he slammed off two shots. Nothing happened with the first, but the second plowed into the man full on, taking him off balance in a staggering fall; and then they were past, crossing the creekbed in a clatter of hooves, lunging full tilt at a brush-fringed ridge rearing up dead ahead.

Through breaking branches and over the crest they went like something shot from a catapult, power in every thrust of those pistoning legs.

104

Parras let the pair run, working off excess energy, that smooth rhythmic stride sweetest music to his ears. "Not likely," he cried, "that bunch'll take after us — doubt if there's anything back there can catch us. Hang on while we open up a little more ground."

He let them run for three minutes, pulled them down to a lope, gradually easing them into a walk. "Which way?" he said, peering, and the girl pointed west.

He could feel her glance digging into his neck and twisted his head to meet the strike of wide eyes. "Well?" he rasped, irritated. "Something stuck in your craw?"

"Did you have to *kill* that fellow back there?"

"You think he come out to play ring around the rosie?"

"Two wrongs," she clipped, "don't set things right!"

Women! he thought, and snatched a grab at his temper. "You can bet we're not the first to sample that neat brand of trickery. Anyways, I didn't kill him; all I done was knock a leg out from under him. He'll live to try that stunt again once he locates more bait for it."

They covered a mile in a kind of cramped silence. He guessed she was trying to sort it all out but he had spoken his piece and any fresh overtures would have to come from her.

A tentative smile, a bit wan but visible, finally crept across her red lips. "You think they make a practice of that?"

"I've quit thinkin'," Parras answered gruffly.

"But . . . "

"You imagine they figured to let us take off with horseflesh like this? An' me with foldin' money still in my jeans?" He looked at her finally. "You told me yourself they'd cut a throat for two bits."

"Guess I did," she said faintly. Then with more vigor, "It will be dark time we get there if we keep on at this rate. Can't we shake it up a little?"

CHAPTER
SIXTEEN

It was dark when they got there. Darker, he thought, than a stack of stove lids, so black Teresa was scarcely a perceptible shadow in a night that was like the inside of a glove.

They were stopped on a slanting, needle-strewn ledge — not, he guessed, entirely sure of their whereabouts. Teresa, nervously peering between cocked ears, huskily whispered, "It *has* to be down there — I mean what's left of it. Can you hear anything?"

"I can hear runnin' water."

"Yes . . . the creek. It comes down the far side and goes out just beneath us — all the excuse for a town those people ever had. Like Cuchillo it was a hideout for rustlers and stage robbers." She let her voice trail away, abruptly asking with a shiver, "Do you suppose Papa's there?"

"We'll find out."

The sound of water rushing through those depths so far below lent an eerie quality to the stillness about them and, again listening into this, Parras asked himself what he was doing here, where he had come from and what had propelled him into problems so obviously having nothing to do with him.

And that business at Cuchillo!

He still marveled at the way he had whipped out that shooter, genuinely astonished when Canvas Coat dropped. He had not guessed he could be that good with a pistol.

He said, mouth tightening, "Let's get off this rim," and kneed his horse forward, letting the sorrel pick its own way, pushing hard on the withers to hold himself back where his weight was less likely to disturb the animal's balance.

He found himself wondering where all this would end. What would become of the girl when he rode off, as he eventually must if he would get to the bottom of his own lost identity? Place to start, like enough, was back there at Lordsburg where he'd picked up those letters . . . or better still, maybe, Shakespeare, where just a few short months ago they had hanged Russian Bill beside Sandy King from the dining room rafters of the Pioneer House.

Gave him kind of a turn to realize suddenly how smoothly the names of that pair and their fate had slipped into his mind like something popped out of a jack-in-the-box. Was his memory beginning to stir at last?

And how did he come to know about this? Had he been there, an eyewitness? Those two had been running with Curly Bill, who was on the black list of Wyatt Earp . . .

This, despite all the try he put into it, was all he was able to dredge up for the moment. In excited frustration he cursed aloud, and Teresa called, "What?"

"Just talkin' to hear my head rattle," he growled, seeing in his mind's eye again the complications of her situation. It did seem like someone had ought to notify the law. But each time his thoughts had come up with this he'd reminded himself he was not these people's keeper.

When you sat right back and really looked at this business, remembering Cuchillo and what Teresa had told him about it, any appeal to local authority would be about as helpful as trying to beller "Dixie" while standing on your head!

What they had around here by all the signs and signal-smokes was that brand of justice contemptuously known as "Yankee law" — less than half a hair different from plain-out self-seeking crookedness.

A man tended to think of his own self as honest, but how honest *was* he? For all Parras knew he could be riding the owlhoot, wanted by half the counties of this or some neighboring territory, running maybe from some Ranger or a Federal marshal's warrant.

It was enough to cramp rats, being saddled with a think-back as maddening as his! He found himself itching to get out those letters in his pocket but this was hardly the time or the place to strike matches. Yanked back, his glance stabbed the roundabout murk of indecipherable shadows, making nothing out of them, marveling that these horses could move so surefootedly through a black thick as this in country unknown to them.

He pulled up with some abruptness in a stand of resinous juniper, saying only to the girl's apprehensive whisper, "We're stickin' here till the moon comes up." No one but a fool would blunder around in this dark. One misstep would put anyone down there on notice.

Sweat came out and lay cold on his neck as he thought what orders might have been given Fay or whoever else might be guarding Don Adolfo. He sure wouldn't put it past that greasy Olivares to have ordered the old man killed if it looked like they might lose him.

He was a little surprised to think he'd come around to accepting the girl's conviction that her dad was still a prisoner. There had been no sign of struggle back there in the old man's room at the ranch. Asleep or drunk he should have put up some resistance; Parras mentioned this now, being careful to keep his voice down.

"But they wanted it to look like Papa had escaped. He was probably unconscious when they took him out of there," Teresa murmured.

Parras nodded in the dark, but still couldn't see what Olivares hoped to gain by this move. It didn't make sense to go to all this bother. Unless something had come up that made it mandatory . . . like perhaps a visit from the law or Sig MacGurdy . . .

Madigan pulled up, his crew behind him, in a thicket of squatting cedars overlooking Two-Pole Pumpkin headquarters. Despite his bold talk he was distinctly uneasy now that it was time to put his reckless impulse irrevocably to the test.

On his right Joel Fay, with an unloaded pistol, sat his horse in fidgeting silence. To the left of the Roman

110

Four owner his range boss, Yorba, enigmatically awaited the word that would commit them.

No one had to tell Madigan how disastrous this could be if Petey's information led them into a trap. Past experience with Olivares' slippery Machiavellian bent gave Madigan no encouragement. He reminded himself it was the chance of a lifetime but kept hearing in his head the deadly racket of hidden rifles.

He tried to shake it off, frustratedly shivering in the breeze that stirred these shaggy branches. It was hard to resist asking Petey to repeat himself, yet he knew there could be no insurance in that. The man would have no reason to lie; what he'd said he believed: that Olivares had taken his whole crew away. But his belief didn't make it so. *That crazy son of a bitch of a Mexican!*

"All right," he growled. "Spread out. We're goin' in."

With clacking bits, the thin tinkle of spur chains, muted thudding of hooves and sundry skreaks of strained leather, the crew moved away to take up fresh stations. "Not *you*," Madigan rasped in the direction of Fay. "I want you right where I can see you — savvy?"

The gunfighter stopped his horse with a sullen snarl.

Madigan took a deep breath, yelling: "*Now!*"

The whole line, running full out, converged on the yard like a charge of cavalry. Sweeping the dark with yells and the *pop pop* of carbines they rounded the house to cut past stables, swung east by the crew shack and hauled up looking foolish — some considerably relieved — before that stupid gringo veranda Romero had tacked on his fortress-like house.

"Reckon Petey called the turn," Yorba said, watching Fay's wiry shape with the sour suspicion through which he viewed most things. In the gloom of this yard he hoped the man might attempt to bolt but Fay, though jumpy as a box filled with crickets, didn't have the kind of guts to embrace such a gamble.

Madigan said to him, "Come on, hotshot. We'll take a look through this place," and got off his horse to step into the deeper black of the veranda.

Fay quit his saddle with extreme reluctance. "Quickest way," he grumbled, "is through that gate yonder . . . "

Madigan, thumping the door, growled, "Where does this go?"

"No place really. All them rooms open off the patio — "

"We'll see. Get up here an' open it."

"Nothin' but a hall," Fay grumbled as he pushed the door open.

"You take the lead. I'll be right behind you," the Roman Four owner said with a fistful of pistol prodding Fay forward down a dark tunnel that opened out to a view of the stars.

"Patio — " Fay said, his jaw suddenly dropping as the door to Don Adolfo's room was thrown open by a night-shirted shape with the shine of a lamp held above its head. "What — "

"Stop right there!" Madigan rapped, the drawn-back hammer of his pistol sounding loud in the tension-ridden silence.

112

The man in the nightshirt raised his lamp higher as though to get the shine of it out of his eyes. "Christ sake, Madigan! What are you up to?"

CHAPTER
SEVENTEEN

It was less dark now beyond the screening juniper as the lopsided bucket of a silver moon crept above rimming peaks. Peering, Parras gradually made out below, midway across a drift of windblown sand, the ruins of what had probably been a file of box-square adobes.

There wasn't much left. Just a tracery of walls, a couple of standing chimneys and part of one building with a fallen-in roof. Fine waste of time this had been, it looked like. Not the least hint of life showed anyplace until a lobo wolf came up out of the creek, thrust its nose at the sky and went ambling off at a hungry prowl across that trackless expanse of sand.

Parras, sorry for the girl, saw no point in talking about it, but continued to watch. Since it was so apparent there was nobody here — no tracks in the sand of that abandoned street and that wolf strolling around like he owned the damned place — why was it, Parras frowningly wondered, that he continued to hang fire sour with his hunger and waste more time on a lost hope like this?

Beside him Teresa stirred restively. She said in a flat kind of all-gone manner, "We're going down there to look, aren't we?"

114

Parras, not answering, continued his surly inspection, still combing his thoughts for the illusive impression that made him keep sweeping that view with his stare.

"Aren't we?" she said, taking hold of his arm.

"You saw that lobo."

"We ought to look anyway. I'd never forgive myself," she said bitterly, "if having come all this way we turned around now without making sure."

Parras was going over in his mind what they'd seen, following that wolf again up from the creek. Hadn't he seemed to be heading first off toward the place where those walls rose so stark from the rest of it? And why, after pointing his nose at the moon, hadn't he barked? Why, instead, had he gone trotting off?

"Do you hear me?" she said, impatiently tightening her grip on his arm.

"I hear you," he answered. She was right about looking. He still couldn't believe there was somebody down there, but he was a lot less sure than he had been. The place was too quiet; this whole area was. He understood now that it had been something about the quality of this silence which had ruffled his nerve ends. He had the feeling of being about to tread on a snake.

The view was much brighter with the moon standing clear and Parras' eyes hunted out ways to come at his objective without alerting the enemy, if possible. He told Teresa, "You stay here."

Dropping out of the saddle he struck off, spider still, by a circuitous route that, while he was longer getting off the slope, kept him in shadow all the way to the moonlit expanse of this deserted street.

From down here the wolf's track plainly showed, and something else that bared Parras' teeth while he drearily stared across the long hundred yards of open sand still between him and the black unfathomable shadow of those walls.

Combing the roundabout terrain from this position, it became all too apparent that the only way he could get nearer without exposing himself was going to take a bit of doing. He would have to cross the creek and come up behind those ruins through a straggle of salt cedars, or stay where he was until the moon got high enough to cooperate. Either course was going to waste more time than he cared to think about.

Had he been alone this wouldn't have mattered, but with a fretful girl left back on that slope, prey to no telling what desperate notions, Parras felt like a man with a bear by the tail — damned either way.

While he was vacillating, trying to think of something better, the play was taken unequivocally away from him. A stone clattered somewhere back up there on the slope. Frozen, cursing breath bitterly caught in his throat, Parras heard the noisy frantic scrambling of a horse trying desperately to keep its balance.

Flame tore whitely from the shadow of those walls and the savage tripled racket of a vomiting rifle fell off the cliffs in wild crescendo. With mounting terror Parras flung himself forward, crazily exposed, pistoning legs digging into the ankles with each floundering lunge through that shifting sand.

Grunting, gasping, impact gap too great for his pistol, with what part of his breath he was able to spare,

116

Parras — trying to distract the sniper from Teresa — lifted his voice in a smothered shout.

He was half across that bright hundred yards when the rifleman, spotting him, spun to his feet and hauled around his weapon, swiveling it belt high to unleash its cargo. Through the blossoming wink of muzzle flash Parras could hear those slugs whimpering past like stirred-up hornets. He was too damned mad and too scared to quit now, and even if he wanted to there wasn't a tuft of grass or a bush big enough in this light to give cover.

If that clown with the rifle had taken time to aim he could have cut Parras off at the knees with that much shooting. The damned fool was rattled but might still get lucky. And not cool enough himself to hold off any longer Parras, flopping where he was, got the sniper in his sights and squeezed off two shots.

The rifleman, yelling, pitched back out of sight.

Still forty yards from the joint of those walls, Parras lunged erect; gasping, and not sure about anything, he went staggering on, gun shoulder high, ready to throw down at the first flutter of movement, eyes stormily fixed to that point of pitch blackness where the fellow had vanished.

And it came within a dime's width of being his undoing.

Less than ten feet from the murk of his objective, the joint of those two walls, some sixth sense hauled his stare hard to the left. So close he could feel the hot flecks of black powder, a reaching spit of flame lanced out, biting into his chest like white iron yanked fresh from the fire.

Off balance, he twisted as he fell, emptying his pistol into that burst in a salvo of concussions that ran on and on like a thunder of bowling balls sending pins flying.

CHAPTER
EIGHTEEN

In the yard at Romero's the Roman Four crew, still in their saddles, uneasily eyed the black hole of that door, stirring restively. Yorba, swinging down in the gabble of voice sounds, jumped for the porch and with lifted gun went lunging across it to bang through the hall and spill into the patio drop-jawed and goggling.

But his astonishment was as nothing to the look that spread across Madigan's features as the nightshirted shape with the lamp fetched it down to show the dispeptic face of Sig MacGurdy.

"I asked," the banker rasped, "what you're doing here, Madigan?"

The Roman Four owner, with Joel Fay stopped against the snout of his six-shooter, looked in that moment fit to bust his surcingle. The blood rushed into his darkening cheeks and the burn of his stare — if looks could kill — should have put MacGurdy in the undertaker's box. "God damn it," he roared, "*you* oughta know what I'm doin' here! With Romero skipped, probably gone into hiding, or so" — prodding Fay — "I've been told by this polecat, I'm naturally here to protect my investment. You got any objection?"

In the face of that glowering scrutiny the banker, though showing some traces of obvious discomfiture, suggested coolly enough, "Seems a little premature, all things considered."

"What's *your* excuse?"

A breathy silence clamped down while the two eyed each other like a pair of strange dogs. "Unless of course," MacGurdy, ignoring this, said through a thin sort of smiling, "you have reason to believe the present owner of record — Don Adolfo — is dead?"

Madigan's stare, narrowing, watched unfavorably through a stillness stretched thinner by unspoken thoughts. The shine of sweat came out on Fay's lip and Yorba's eyes in that self-certain face were alive with hostility when Indigo Wells shoved open the gate in a jingle of spurs to sardonically drawl: "Somebody comin'. What you want we should do?"

When the din rolled away Parras was minded to get himself up and go look for the girl; some survival mechanism, though, developed through times he could not remember, held him stiff in cramped placement for another drag of heart thumps while stretched ears tested the quality of this quiet and hard eyes probed the black depths of shadow cast by the juncture of those two standing walls.

The night refused to divulge its secrets and if anyone else was waiting back of that shadow no suggestion of movement was apparent to confirm this.

He could feel a wet stickiness creeping over his chest and pain like the cut of a knife followed hard on the

120

heels of each breath he drew. He was pressed by the need of doing something about this, yet held where he was against the cushioning sand by the dangers inherent in the possibility of more than just two of Olivares' crew being here. Or was it just the one — that fellow he'd lost track of after the first exchange of shots?

That first one had a rifle. The gun which had managed to knock Parras down had sounded more like a hogleg, though he guessed it could have been the same finger.

He felt like a goddam goldfish, exposed in this light with an empty pistol. If Romero was back there and still in the quick you'd have thought he'd have been heard from, yet what other reason could account for the trigger-happy antics which had brought on this gunplay?

"Are you all right, Parras?"

The concern in her voice did not warm Parras any. With his head in the sand he continued to explore the edgy silence around him, striving to detect faintest hint of breath or movement, hearing nothing . . . convinced any worry she felt had more to do with her father than with any kind of fretting occasioned by himself.

Horse sounds intruded, blocking out the things he listened for, nervously moving nearer, stopping then advancing as she sniffed the night for danger.

"God damn it," he rasped, "ain't you got a lick of sense!" He pushed himself up, disgustedly coming onto his knees to punch empty shells from his shooter, his stare continuing to probe blue shadows as he thumbed fresh loads into the still warm cylinder.

Eyes sliding irascibly through the fluttering shadows he got onto his feet and, gun held ready, stepped gingerly closer to the ragged joint of half ruined walls, slipping back of the nearest to advance obliquely into the deeper black of that murk. When still nothing happened he struck a match, holding it cupped above his head to peer a long moment before moving out of her sight.

The girl, dropping from the saddle with a bright flash of leg, ground-hitched the two horses and, shying away from a crumpled shape, sped hurriedly after him.

Near the vee of those walls, stark in the matchflame, lay a second sprawled shape: the sniper who had tried to cut her down with his rifle. Teresa's stare widened; then she hastened to where Parras was bent over, cutting the old man loose of his bonds.

"Have they killed him? Is he dead?" she gasped, bending nearer.

The pale whiskered face certainly gave that impression. The burned-down match fizzled out and Parras, getting a fresh one out of his hatband, whipped it alight. Reaching it out, he bade her hold it up where he could see.

Cut loose of the ropes Don Adolfo did not look any better but Parras, considering him, finally grunted, "He don't look to've been shot. Probably one of 'em clonked him over the head when they heard you moving around with those horses. Don't look like he's hurt much, except for that bump, I mean," he tacked

122

on when he felt the jerk of her eyes digging into him. "Probably shock, mostly."

She snapped, "Shock can kill when you get to be his age!"

"You suggestin'," Parras growled, "we ought to camp out here?"

"How can we move him when — "

"We'll move him. Make no mistake about that. We've got to," Parras threw at her grimly, "if you figure to keep Olivares away from him. It's dollars to doughnuts he's on his way here right now."

Flame licked at her fingers and she dropped the match, but not before he observed the pale set of her angry features. He got up and turned away, not minded to argue, saying over his shoulder, "You wait right here — and this time stay put or you can find someone else to do your gunfightin' for you."

Southwest of their position, ten miles by crow flight, the dark silhouettes of several Chihuahua-hatted horsemen crested a ridge and drew rein to blow their mounts. With a leg around the horn Olivares, settling back, produced a sack of Durham and twisted up a smoke. Only four of his crew were with him; less trusted members had been left behind to throw up a pretense of searching for Romero, cannily coached in a tale sardonically intended to display their loyalty to the brand and absent owner.

This attention to detail was the mayordomo's strength and weakness. He had never been prone to put trust in luck, having learned early how deceitful this could be. He hadn't got where he was by leaving things to chance where he could find any way of coppering his bets.

Which was why just now he told the biggest hombre, "Luis, take Felix and Pepe and go 'round across the Mimbres and drop into that canyon from the south; you got that straight?"

"*Seguro*. Sure. But why?" Luis asked, his puzzlement plain.

"Because," Olivares answered — then stopped with a shrug, saying softly, "Let's just call it insurance. Get going."

CHAPTER
NINETEEN

Confirming his conviction that there was no one else around, Parras found three horses tied among the willows darkly fringing the creek's far bank.

When he got them out where he could see what these looked like all three proved to be branded Two-Pole Pumpkin. While this did not greatly surprise him he had been rather hoping to turn up something tying the Roman Four owner into this deal. Madigan's contribution to Olivares' bold plan to take the old man's ranch away from him was apparently limited to disposal of the stock both outfits were stealing.

Parras, although confident Olivares had one, could not come up with any down-to-earth reason why the man would encourage — much less take part in — stripping an outfit he hoped to make his own. Of course the rustling may have been instigated before Romero's mayordomo let out his loop to embrace this larger steal. Whatever the understanding between those two it was bound at best to be, like most thieves' arrangements, an uneasy alliance with neither of them likely to trust the other out of sight.

There ought to be some sort of advantage to this if a man could just latch onto the right lever. Both of them had their sights firmly set on taking over the ranch, each warily ready to double-cross the other at first opportunity.

Considering, he couldn't see much chance of the girl ever managing to come out on top. She had no one but him to count on and no way he could see of putting a crew together.

Parras grunted, disgusted, a damned white chip in a no limit game.

Part of this outlook, he tried to tell himself, came of being bone weary and going too many hours of strain and activity without putting anything into his belly.

But the fact remained that he was just one man. He loosed a curse beneath his breath in a kind of desperate anger that he should be in this at all. If he'd a quarter of the sense God gave gophers he'd cut loose and climb out of this jackpot right now!

Deep inside, though, he knew a bitter futility. Even if he put his own hide first, prepared — which he wasn't — to abandon Teresa, nobody was going to let him ride out. He was in too far, a marked man now. Both sides would be gunning for him.

The futility reminded him of cold mornings on his father's ranch, doing chores they couldn't afford to hire done, patching things with baling wire, unable even to scrape up the cash to send his mother to a doc who might have saved her. Years of grinding misery on a backbreaking two-by-four spread backed into the roughs where even wild horses had been unable to subsist.

126

He was half across the moonlit sand, preoccupied with frustration, when the realization hit him. Stopped in his tracks, stiffly holding the reins of the horses, he tried to force remembrance — anything to widen the crack suddenly opened on that mist-locked past.

It availed him nothing. No new bit came through. He could not discover where his father's place was, where it had been or if he still had it. He could not even recall his father's name — either one of them.

Snarling in exasperation he dragged the snorting, half spooked horses up to the broken walls of the covert. Almost as ill-humored as Parras felt, Teresa called from the dark, "What makes you so sure they're going to come out here? I should think — "

"*Somebody's* got to. You take a look at their gear? No grub left at all. If you been thinking Olivares would be a fool to come near here you're probably right, but he'd have to manage to keep these boys fed. Hired guns wouldn't figure to stick long without grub no matter what deal they made, and Olivares would know it. The clincher's your father."

She came out of the shadow, peering, uncertain. "How do you mean?"

"He's gone to a heap of bother to set up the notion your father bolted. He wouldn't want anything to upset that and you can bet your bottom dollar he's not about to take any chances. That you might talk is a risk he'll take, figurin' to sew you into double harness. But the old man shootin' off his mouth? He can't afford that."

Parras turned away, quickly stripping the halters from the mounts that had brought them to this desolate place. He stepped past her then, deeper into the black, to return with the rifle and a pocketful of cartridges salvaged from the sniper. Two of the three horses fetched from the creek had no saddle guns on them and he shoved the rifle into the nearer mount's scabbard, then strode past the girl again to bring out the old man.

When he started with Romero toward the rifleless horse the girl jumped in front of him, barring his path. She cried, choked with feeling: "You can't put him on a horse like that!"

"Why not?"

"He's still unconscious — "

"I can take care of that. We got plenty of rope," Parras growled, starting around her.

With eyes like two holes burned in a bedsheet Teresa sprang in front of him again. "Is there no humanity in you at all?" She spat at him fiercely: "He's my father, damn you! He's in no condition to be roped to a saddle!"

Parras, scowling, shifted weight. "You figure to carry him piggyback maybe?" Fed up with her tantrums, he said in clipped tones, "He goes roped to a saddle or he don't go at all. Either way I'm gettin' out of this place."

They stood locked in outrage, both of them glaring.

It was the girl who sulkily stepped back finally.

Parras tied the old man facedown, wrists to ankles, tested the ropes to make sure he was secure, the girl watching bitterly. When he turned she caught sight of the blood and put out a hand, shocked stare filled with horror. "You've been shot!"

128

"I'll live," he growled, dragging hands across pantslegs. He caught up the reins and put them into her fist. Moving around her then he grabbed up another pair, thrust a boot in the stirrup and was about to swing up when a clatter of hooves sounded sharp against stone, heard even through the purl of the babbling creek.

Back in the patio at Romero headquarters Madigan, twisting, flung up his head, snarling, "Who — *how many?*" while the nightshirted banker, still frozen to his lamp, peered from one to the other before staring gateward in almost comical alarm.

"Better look for yourself," grumbled Indigo Wells. He turned as Madigan joined him to poke out a hand toward the moon-bathed corrals.

"I don't see nothin'," Madigan rasped.

His hired gunfighter nodded. "Cagey," he said. "I ain't seen 'em yet, neither, but there's somebody out there. Three, four of them, sounded like."

Madigan peered at his crew, some mounted, some standing, all of them staring toward the poles of the pens. "Olivares, you think?"

Indigo shrugged. "That's what I figured till I saw that damn Yankee."

"MacGurdy?"

"Who else? What's that money-grabber doin' here?"

Madigan, scowling, chewed his lip, then made up his mind. "Whatever it is," he rasped, "it ain't goin' to work! Get out there an' tell them boys to take cover!

We've got this place an' by Gawd we'll keep it! Slug the first sonofabitch that comes into your sights!"

He slammed the gate behind Wells and, spinning, bumped into Yorba; he shoved him off in a splutter of oaths. "Where's that damn Fay?" He glared and, cursing, pushed past to catch hold of the banker, shaking him, bellering, "Where'd he go?"

The frightened MacGurdy almost dropped his lamp. "In — in there," he quavered, pointing hand trembling. "Romero's office . . . "

Even as Madigan dived for the door a bullet plowed through it, narrowly missing, to smash like the strike of a fist somewhere back of him. Staring at that splintered hole in the door the Roman Four owner with dropped jaw stood rooted till a second slug drove him cursing to cover.

CHAPTER
TWENTY

Parras' whole body stiffened in that one-footed stance, every fiber of him rigid as he stared toward the creek and that blue murk of shadow where the willows overhung it, clenched fist choking the horn so fiercely it seemed to the girl he never would let go of it. A muscle began to jerk in his chest.

Without moving his eyes from that skewering look, he muttered, "We're going to have to run for it. Cut for the brush. Go on — *get cracking!*"

With an inarticulate gasp she sprang to the saddle, beating her heels against the flanks of her mount, the horse packing Romero dragged snorting after her; and still Parras hung there, hard eyes searching the dark, his free hand drawing the Winchester from its scabbard, waiting to give her all the start he could manage.

Not till he heard a cursing yell did he pull himself up to throw a leg across the cantle; crouched there, peering, gnawed by hunger growling deep in his belly and the swiveling wildness of exasperated tensions, till he saw that bright burst of flame in the darkness, hammering two slugs at the quivering heart of it, the shout tearing sharp through widening clamor. Not until then did he dig in the steel to go — stretched like an Indian — barreling after her.

She was already lost in the brush of the slope when he sent the fresh horse leaping powerfully at it, feeling the grab of those pistoning hooves.

Shoving the rifle under his leg Parras braced himself with boots hard in the oxbows as they streaked like an avalanche through breaking branches to come at the incline and surge scrambling upward in great lunging jumps.

Coming onto the bench where they'd stopped coming down he hauled up a moment, twisting around to look back, scrinched eyes almost shut as he peered through this dark pungent shagginess of junipers. There was nothing in sight near that tumbled-down ruin but closer, hard under him, crossing that strip of moon-white sand, a solitary horseman was quirting his mount like hell wouldn't have him.

Parras lifted the rifle. With the butt against shoulder he leveled and paused. When he led that hurtling shape again he threw off a little before squeezing the trigger. The horse went down in a staggering fall. Parras tight-mouth, turned his own, went on with less hurry, not satisfied really but confident enough they'd gain at least a quarter hour while that fellow down there was hunting up another mount.

It loomed large in his thoughts that they could not ram around through these hills indefinitely without courting disaster; sooner or later the odds would run them into a trap — most probably one he couldn't shoot his way out of.

He cursed under his breath. He didn't like shooting horses. He didn't like shooting men, but that could be rationalized. He found it harder to excuse gunning down a defenseless horse. Calling it a larger target didn't help much.

He pushed on, rimming out to find the girl waiting.

They looked at each other in this pale light, neither of them particularly comfortable. Parras swung down to have a look at Don Adolfo, finding the old man still unconscious. Anyone could see this wasn't doing him any good.

"Where do we go now?" Teresa asked gruffly.

Parras, rubbing his jaw, said, "There must be some kind of law in this country . . . "

"*Gringo* law!" she spat in contempt. "Do you think any Texican would help my father?"

Having no answer Parras checked the old man's fastenings and got back in the saddle, angrily aware of the passing time, frantically knowing they couldn't afford to stand still. "We sure as hell can't go back to the ranch . . . " Remembering something, he reached into his shirt pocket, feeling the stickiness of blood on his hand.

She saw him staring at it, said with decision, "We better have a look at that."

He jerked his head up. "Later." He sounded like his mind was a hundred miles away. She watched him rub again at the stubble of beard along one cheek. Still with that far-off queerness he asked, "Think you could manage to get us to Shakespeare?"

"I never heard of — "

"What about Lordsburg?"

"What do you want to run way off down there for?"

"We got to run someplace and — "

"Why?"

He spoke to her bluntly. "If Olivares gets his hands on Don Adolfo again he'll kill him. He's not in this for marbles — Madigan, either. We can't hole up around here, not without grub, not the way this is shaping."

"There are closer places . . . "

"You've answered that already. If the law works for gringos we've got to get out of here."

"But Lordsburg's clean the other side of the Burrows!"

"That's bad?"

"It wouldn't be easy . . . "

"Nothing's like to be easy in this kind of jackpot! There's a chance if you can get us to Lordsburg I might pick up some sort of help." He said, plainly impatient, "You better make up your mind before that feller gets up here."

With another long look but without further words she picked up her reins and led off, angling southwest down the spine of this spur.

Parras swung his mount in behind Don Adolfo, wishing the night were considerably darker but thankful that at least they were moving through timber: it might screen them for a while. But that ranny he'd put afoot was probably mounted by now and when he got up here — if he wasn't a plumb fool — he'd hang fire till he spotted them. Which he could do right enough when they rode into the open off down there below. You could see a far piece against sand in this light.

Abruptly, ahead of him, Teresa pulled up.

Following the point of her outstretched arm he glimpsed a huddle of riders coming out of the south. Parras' mouth tightened. From this height and distance they might have been coyotes, but there was no doubt about it: they were bound for this spur. He counted three, waved a hand. "Get moving. Shake it up."

She had to give him an argument. "You don't know — "

"I know well enough we got no friends around here. Whoever they are they'll be no help to us. Get humpin'!" he cried at her, kicking his own mount.

"But won't they see us?"

"They sure as hell will if we don't get out of this." He ranged up alongside. "That big grulla," he muttered, "looks like one of your father's," and cut her horse with his rein ends, whacking the other as she broke into a lope.

From this point the land rolled sharply downward through thinning trees into second growth stuff and finally brush to come out on the open emptiness of desert. Already their cover was running out of concealment value but the riders below hadn't altered course which, to the girl anyway, indicated she and Parras might slip past undetected. Parras himself wasn't counting on this. Old in the ways of pursuit and flight, he wasn't about to take anything for granted. He kept his eyes narrowly peeled, twisting around in the saddle to follow their course as the three below got into brush and put reluctant mounts to the climb.

Now well past any probability of a head-on collision Parras and the girl, running at right-angles, should be into the desert before that outfit reached hailing distance of the remounted man, but Parras was not breathing easy yet. Until those three got considerably higher they could change course and, nearer the desert Parras hoped to get lost in, close the gap too fast for comfort. Even fresh horses — if they were spotted too soon — couldn't put that bunch out of rifle range fast enough to guarantee safety.

There were clouds in the sky, one of these directly in line with the moon but too many minutes away from concealing it to do them much good.

Parras, fervently praying their luck would hang on, used his rein ends again as they came out of second growth and dashed for the dark line of brush ahead of them that screened these footslopes from the desert beyond.

The next time he twisted his neck to look up the moon wasn't more than six breaths from that cloud. They banged into the brush with a crash of snapped branches and just as he was beginning to think they had it made something sailed past his ear like a hornet.

CHAPTER
TWENTY-ONE

Madigan, furiously crouched behind the mortared coping that topped Romero's patio well, ground his teeth as he glared at the door to the old man's office behind which Fay had so desperately taken cover.

But, a larger issue presently remembered, he abruptly jumped up, putting the man out of mind. Olivares' gunfighter wasn't going anywhere through the barred slits of the windows in this place.

With Indigo's words ringing through his head the Roman Four owner faced the man with the lamp, scowling anew as he took in the nightshirt, recognizing its significance. That son of a bitch Yankee had made himself right to home!

"I'll have the truth of it, MacGurdy; you better speak out. You didn't come out here all the way from Socorro just to swap bull with a goddam Mex!"

The banker licked at pale lips. He had to try twice just to get out a mumble, but when he saw Madigan's hand begin to move beltward he sprang into speech. "I came out here to get a count on those cattle!"

"You know," Madigan said through a thin kind of smiling, "for a twittery old fool that ain't half bad. But since you sold me them notes what happens to the cattle ain't no skin off your — "

"But that's just it," MacGurdy protested. "When you took over those notes it *made* the matter of their numbers *my* responsibility." He walled his eyes in a quiet that seemed to have become strangely loud. He cried, swallowing nervously: "I came out here to make sure you got what you paid for!"

"I bet."

Madigan, nodding, pushed the ball of a thumb across the bite of gold-flashing molars while cold eyes tracked a darkening stare from bare, shoeless feet to the disheveled wisps of the man's sparse hair. "You go over that enough you might even get to believe it."

"As God's my witness — " the banker quavered, but the cowman's production of a long-barreled pistol left the rest of that remark hung up in his throat.

"If you don't want to find a breeze blowin' through you," Madigan said with the knell of doom, "you better sound convincin' pretty all-fired quick."

With MacGurdy goggling like a fish out of water the ranchman thumbed back the hammer of his pistol.

"Wait — " the frightened man frantically gasped, but in that precise moment a racket of rifles tore the night wide open and Madigan, cursing, spun to leap toward the gate, the cow boss, Yorba, hard on his heels.

They burst into a yard that seemed completely empty, peering scrinch-eyed through a drift of black powdersmoke to where a prone kicking horse midway down the lane lay close by two smaller lumps of motionless flesh.

138

The Roman Four leather slapper, Wells, came out from behind a corner of the smithy to stroll with jingling spurs across the interval to join them. With a rifle held loosely in the crook of an arm he jerked his chin toward the dying horse.

"Got a rough edge or two," he noted with callous indifference, "but a pretty fair job considerin' the light." He showed a cat's grin. "You can be damn sure the jigger that got away won't be burnin' up his axles in no hurry to come back."

The rest of the Roman Four outfit began to filter out of the night's blacker shadows. Madigan said, "Let's take a look at them," and set off up the lane, the other two following.

One of the pair beside the horse lay facedown with an arm doubled under him; the other, twisted onto his side, lay sightlessly staring from open eyes. Both were obviously dead.

As Yorba rolled the nearest onto his back with an out-thrust boot a bit of metal on the vest threw out a flash of reflected light. Madigan leaning forward, stiffened.

"Jesus Christ!" he said in a rush, and pulled over the other man, bitterly swearing. "You know what you've done?" he cried in a fury, twisting his head to glare up at Wells.

"I done what you told me," Indigo answered. "Is it my fault the bugger turned out to be sheriff?"

"Quick!" Parras shouted. "Feed the steel to that bronc!" and spurred up alongside as they broke from the brush to belt the pack horse with the flat of his Winchester. "We'll have to run for it!"

If there was one thing he understood better than any other it was that here was no time to be sparing of horseflesh. This hellity larrup wasn't like to be doing Romero any good but there was no help for that. There was no sign of cover — not even a bush, just this damned fluted sand laying in waves like some petrified ocean. They had to keep going. They had to pull further away or be shot into dollrags.

And that other john, too, would be after them now.

"We better run for the ranch," Teresa called back at him, but Parras shook his head.

That was probably what these rannies were expecting them to do. He weighed this possibility for factors which might widen the gap, increasing their lead, but there were none he would bank on. If the pursuit could be thoroughly sold on this notion they might split up, a couple of them maybe dogging the trail while the third hombre tried to effect a shortcut. But Parras was skeptical: as long as those jaspers could see their quarry they were going to hang on, doing their best to come into rifle range again.

This was the big danger Parras had to guard against, the reason he was pushing so hard right now. Three-to-one was poor odds from his side of the table, and it could easily be four. To be sure he had Teresa but in his estimation this was like to be more handicap than help, and the old man was no kind of card to draw to.

It looked like all he could draw to was a busted flush!

They had to hold their lead and increase it, 'cause it didn't look like losing those rannies was going to be anything a feller could hope for. If hope was in order he'd better hope for a miracle — that moon wasn't going to be out of sight long.

They say speak of the devil and the devil appears. He'd been thinking of hope and now he was given some. Five minutes out of that foothill brush they dropped over the bank of one of those channels dug by the runoff from cloudbursts, plunging, wildly skidding on crumpling earth. It was just like the ground had opened up to swallow them.

Twelve feet down they came onto firm bottom and a good chance to stretch out their lead a few rope lengths; and the moon like it was laughing shook free of the clouds to light their way. When the pursuers got here they wouldn't know till they got down to the business of hunting out tracks which way Parras and the girl had gone, back into the foothills or south toward the border.

They would be more likely to head for the border, and that was the way Parras told her to go. Southwest of them someplace was Deming and Lordsburg and he sure didn't want to get jammed in these hills again.

He spun horse, pulling up, to urge the others ahead of him, slapping their mounts with the slack of his reins, turning left back of them, crowding, almost shoving them down that dry, shale-strewn course with no regard for the clatter, intent only on putting as many of this gully's snake-like twists between their tails and pursuit as possible. "Pick it up — pick it up!" he growled, harrying them on.

He was more and more surprised by the urges or know-how that shaped these decisions . . . a kind of intuition he couldn't believe in for a moment.

This sixth sense, or whatever, seemed a heap more to him like second nature, chain reactions compounded of things gone into so often no thinking was necessary; and he scowled at this notion, suspecting uncomfortably these were old ingrained habits developed in a past that was still irascibly just out of reach.

He didn't ask what sort of habits could have engendered such a sharpness, but an awareness of this caginess kept poking and gnawing at the edges of his conscience, which had not been concerned at all with those gone men he'd put his gun on. This hard core which seemed to underlie all his actions, like the practical considerations of tying Romero to the back of that jouncing horse, was not a thing a man cared to dwell on. It rather tended to make Parras irritably wonder if the past he had forgotten wasn't better left buried.

CHAPTER
TWENTY-TWO

The Roman Four owner, bitterly staring at the shine of badge on the dead man's chest, was in a turmoil of confusion. He could not escape his jittery thoughts nor scrape them together to make a decision with so many new worries suddenly confronting him.

He couldn't possibly accept responsibility for this. He could bury these stiffs, pack them someplace else and stomp down a cutbank to hide his guilt, but that might not prove good enough. Almost certainly the sheriff would have left word somewhere or mentioned to somebody what he was up to — and you couldn't pack off that goddam horse!

And what about that other one: the deputy these fools had let get away? By morning the whole countyseat would be buzzing; the law wasn't going to just write this thing off! What you did to a Mex around here was one thing, what you did to the law in the person of its sheriff was a different kettle of fish entirely. Every nut and his uncle would show up with a firearm when the law came back to deal out retribution.

Yorba, whose thoughts must have coursed the same channel, said, "We've got to git outa here!"

"What the hell good will that do?" Madigan spluttered, loath in spite of everything to give this place up. "The feller that got away — "

"He didn't see nobody," Wells growled defensively.

"That's right," declared Yorba with all the authority of a man who'd seen nothing. "Alls he can say is they rode into the yard here an' all hell broke loose. Romero'll take the blame; no one can prove we ever been near the place. It's him they'll be after, figurin' that's why he dug for the tules." He dredged up a grin.

It was not shared by Madigan. "And what you reckon he'll say when they latch onto him?"

"Mebbe they won't," Wells chipped in, surprisingly thoughtful. "A Mexican is lyin' fore he opens his mouth. Who's gonna believe 'im? Special with the evidence buried right in his yard!" He said to Yorba, "Let's plant 'em under them horse turds piled up back of the stables."

"Be safer to bury them — " Yorba began, but his boss broke in with a pitying snort. "We *want* them found, don't we? Sooner they swing that crackpot Adolfo the quicker we pick up what's left of this outfit. With the notes I've bought off that — " His eyes suddenly bulged. Without bothering to finish he started up the lane toward the house. "Go ahead — dig 'em in," he called back over a shoulder, and pulled up to curse.

"What's the matter?" Yorba growled, coming up on the run. Madigan swiveled a look across the yard. Lowering his voice he rasped like it was taking the dollars right out of his pocket, "That sonofabitchin' banker's the joker that fetched them peckernecks out

144

here! Hidin' them ain't goin' to help us none — not with *him* knowin' . . . "

Even in this poor light it was plain to be seen that the Roman Four mogul wasn't more than two jumps from coming apart at the seams. The avalanche of sudden reverses was rapidly sweeping him toward a state of near hysteria. He obviously didn't know which way to turn, hung up in his tracks standing there glaring, about as groggy as a poleaxed steer.

This unexpected display of human weakness put new life into the sandy-haired Yorba. "Hell, that pile's big enough to hide all three o 'em; let Indigo take care of him. I'll put some of the boys to shiftin' it straightaway. No trouble at all, an' while they're at it Deuce an' Nevada can dig a hole for that nag. We don't have to move him. They can plant him where he's at."

Madigan pulled up his chin. He liked this solution but you could see he was afraid of it. "You can't just take a son of a bitch like him and dump him in a hole. The man's a banker, goddam it — there'll be all kinds of talk!"

"So let 'em talk." Yorba grinned. "When he's found with the sheriff folks'll know who to blame. You go find yourself someplace to set down. You got a partner now, remember?"

Madigan, still grumbling and scowling like a man caught in a hitch he couldn't quite get his hands on, went muttering off in the direction of the corrals.

He slumped his weight against a pole, settling there filled with his broody thoughts. He flinched, uncontrollably shuddering when the sound of a shot set all his

145

nerve ends twanging. He certainly hadn't figured when he let Olivares talk him into this hoedown — into rustling a few steers — that it was liable to wind up like this. Killing sheriffs and bankers . . . Where would it end?

But as Yorba's talk came back to him he began to perk up. The man was right about Romero: nobody was going to believe the old fool, running off like he had. Maybe this was going to work out after all. What he ought to do, probably, was head for the countyseat with that pocketful of notes he had bought from MacGurdy and —

He jumped away from the pole with a curse. He knew now what they'd forgotten! Breaking into a run, he was half across the yard when Yorba called out: "All set. You ready to ride?"

Ignoring him, Madigan plunged on. Shoving open the massive, iron-strapped gate he charged into the moonlit patio, pulling up, goggle eyed, to stare in disbelief.

"Christ sake, Madigan! You gone off your rocker?" Yorba grumbled, catching up with him.

"*Where is he?*"

"Where's who?"

With a cold sweat glistening on his ashen cheeks Madigan pointed a shaking hand at the wide open door of Don Adolfo's office.

"Joel Fay . . . " He gasped like the ground was breaking up under him.

CHAPTER
TWENTY-THREE

Bad as Madigan's outlook was, it was scarcely more desperate than the prospect faced by Polito Olivares when horse shot from under him, he glared up at those brush-darkened slopes that had hidden his last glimpse of Teresa, Walt Parras and the departing hostage from whom he'd every reason to believe he could wring a ranch.

That *borracho* old man had been his ace in the hole against the mushrooming greed of that Texican, Madigan, he'd so blithely dealt in to hasten Romero's downfall. He was stunned by the magnitude of this double-barreled catastrophe which, at a single stroke, had nullified the advantages it had taken him months to consolidate. Outraged by the picture of his assets galloping away behind the guns of that damned gringo, Olivares whirled to break into a run, bound for the horse of his dead companion.

He'd been on the right track when he'd knocked Parras' horse over Tenkiller that time, but the man had the luck of ten thousand devils! When he'd shown up the next morning at Two-Pole Pumpkin Olivares should have shot him out of hand, girl or no fool girl, by God. Sparing that Anglo had been his greatest mistake, but

147

he still had a crew and he still had the ranch, and in this remote region the man in possession had a lot going for him. A case could be dragged through the courts till half those concerned —

He pulled up, panting, glaring. What the hell was he doing, charging around like a rooster after chickens with their heads off! He was Polito Olivares, who had always taken pride in letting others do the running. Besides, he still had his insurance, the men he'd sent to cut off escape south, big Luis, Felix, Pepe; surely the three of them could stop one gringo!

But he wasn't as sure as he would like to have been.

He spun into another cursing run but the sound and look of him spooked Sancho's horse, which took off, head high, back of dangling reins. Olivares was so wild he almost shot the fool critter. He had to choke down his rage and in pretended indifference putter around like his whole damned future wasn't at stake until the fool nag had quieted enough for Olivares to get hold of him. He finally bagged him with a handful of creek sand rattled in a pan. By then he was in no fit mood to ride anything. He knew this was folly but, too wild to care, he quirted the eye-rolling, terrified brute all the way to the top of that stiff woodsy slope.

Rimming out he lashed the wheezing horse on across the tree-covered bench until they came to where he could overlook the cloud-darkened desert.

He had thought he heard shots while crossing the bench but could see no wink of muzzleflash anywhere. No cricket sound even. Nothing came through the

148

lunging pant of his horse but the push of the wind through needled branches.

He fiddled with impatience, straining his eyes in this blue murk of starshine, frantic to be off yet held by the need to know what was unfolding in the dark immensity of terrain spread below.

When the moon shook free to catch up the desert in its silvery wash he was barely in time to see a huddle of horsebackers drop out of sight as completely and sudden as the cold gleam of chalkmarks sponged from a slate.

He could translate that into a gorge or dry wash snaking off through the desert. His glimpse of the riders had been so brief that he couldn't guess with any certainty if those had been his men or Parras and party.

He kicked the horse into motion, quirt hanging idle as they dropped down the spur with his thoughts jumping around like a boxful of hoppers.

There was no way of telling where that damned wash went in this trustless light. One thing he could do whoever he had seen: he could chase along the rim of that gully, skipping the twists, and maybe get ahead of them if this stupid damn horse could hold out long enough.

Back at the ranch Yorba, too, was caught in the grip of frenzied dreads, but he put these aside to make sure the man had indeed flown the coop. Fay was gone, all right; Romero's office was empty — but this was no proof the man had gotten clear. He could still be in reach, and even if he wasn't how far would an idjit like him get afoot?

Always one for ironing things out by the most direct route, Yorba plunged down the dark hall and yelled from the veranda to find out if the crew had any mounts missing. It was discovered they had. Nevada, after a brief confusion, turned out to be the goat in this deal, Wells sarcastically suggesting it probably wouldn't hurt him to throw a leg over the horse MacGurdy had come on. "A dead man's bronc?" Nevada cried squakily. "Not on your tintype!"

The cow boss had better and more urgent things to do than stand around listening to that brand of guff. "It don't make me no never-mind what you ride. Just get to hell into a saddle an' start beatin' the bushes — the bunch of you!"

Wells asked curiously, "What's up, boss?"

"That goddam halfbreed Fay has took off!"

This brought on a gabble of comment that Yorba sheared off like a passing train. "If you're countin' on warmin' the backs of your asses in Roman Four linecamps come snow-fly git out there an' find him. I want that whippoorwill stopped! Them as don't hanker to have any part in it can step up an' draw your time right now!"

That sent the whole outfit into their saddles, at which point Yorba had a final word for them. "Don't come back here — you got that? Shut his mouth when you find him an' git back to that cow hunt. We got a roundup to finish an' we ain't got all fall."

Originally, this wash had seemed just the miracle Parras had been praying for. Now he wasn't so sure. They did not seem, to his worried notion, to be making as good time down here dodging boulders.

This wouldn't matter too much so long as the pursuit hung hard on their sign; but if that trigger-happy trio, instead of bothering with tracks, had been smart enough to stay out of this gully and lope along its rim, then there could be a hereafter for someone mighty soon.

And the hell of it was these damn banks had grown steeper, affording no chance to climb out of this now. It was too late to turn back. All that was left was to keep pushing on with what speed they could manage, hoping this gorge would play out before that bunch coming after them could get into gun range.

The prospect of being shot like fish in a barrel wasn't the kind of thing to shore up sagging spirits. The freshness of their horses was no advantage at all down here and the acumen of hindsight wasn't any great help either. And telling himself he should have had more sense did not materially advance their chances. Parras lifted the rifle again from under his leg, toying with the notion of trying to stand them off while the girl and her father pushed on to get clear.

It probably wouldn't work, even if he was minded to stick his neck out that way. It was Teresa and Romero who had brought those hombres after them — they wouldn't care about Parras. So unless those jaspers had dropped into the wash any rearguard action he sought to set up was not going to amount to a hill of beans. If they were skirting the rim they'd go right on past; and also to be remembered was that pelican Parras had set afoot. You could damn well bet he'd be mounted again!

Rack his mind as he would and bitterly did, the only solution he could find to this jackpot was to keep right on with what they were doing.

He had no idea how many miles had unreeled since they'd got into this fix, probably not over two. It might reasonably play out before they covered another and whether they were caught down here or not in the open didn't seem in the long run to make much difference. It was bound to wind up in gunplay, regardless. And, unless they found cover, he saw but one end in sight.

CHAPTER
TWENTY-FOUR

Then, suddenly, they got lucky.

As they rounded another of its innumerable turns, the floor of the gulch took an upward slant and they were bent forward, climbing. Within a hundred yards this pitch grew sharper, walls abruptly drooping away until Parras, peering ahead, glimpsed a jumble of silvered and purple hills reaching up through the night.

It took some realizing. Then they were crossing that stretch of blown sand, Parras deeply breathing after twisting his head to find no one behind him. It was almost like feeling whole years roll away — not that he was naïve enough to imagine they were safe. He knew better than to think Romero's troubles had packed up and gone home. Somewhere, unseen, men armed with guns would be still grimly seeking. But now, barely minutes away from those hills, Parras was able to hope there might yet be a chance.

Now that some of the pressures had slackened a little Parras was reminded to give some tag ends of thought to the man who had been Olivares' prisoner.

Hatless, helpless, folded head-down across the jounce of that saddle, this wild rush through the night couldn't have done him much good; but, short of abandoning him, there'd been no other choice.

This did not very greatly lessen Parras' discomfiture. Whatever their differences — and there had obviously been some — it was natural Teresa would resent seeing her father bandied about like a sack of potatoes.

He could feel her stiff, silent displeasure like a weight hanging around him. He couldn't think why her opinion or cockeyed notions should make any difference one way or the other but after another couple looks at their backtrail he reluctantly growled at the girl to pull up.

Quitting the saddle, he untied Romero and lifted the old man out onto the sand. He looked pretty puny in this unconscious state and the rasp of his breathing was not encouraging. The girl, hurrying up, shouldered Parras aside, bending to put a hand on her parent, kneeling to take the man's head in her lap with a mutter of Spanish that shut Parras out.

He checked the horses, found them in better shape than he'd a right to expect. Hearing the mumble of the old man's voice Parras rejoined them. Romero had his eyes open. "Think he can manage to sit a horse now?" Parras asked dubiously.

Struggling onto an elbow Romero answered for himself. "Of course!" But the old tone of arrogance simply wasn't there. Pride had pushed those words out. Parras didn't think pride would keep him in the saddle but he wasn't going to argue if that was what they wanted.

154

He helped Teresa get the man on his feet and could feel the weakness in trembling limbs. Without comment Parras put out a hand to help him into the saddle, but the old man wouldn't take his help. Shaking off the hand he got a foot in the stirrup and pulled himself aboard, grunting, to look down at the gringo with a fierce satisfaction.

Teresa cried out in fright and Parras, head jerked across shoulder, saw the dark shapes of riders spewing out of the gulch.

A cold knot turned over somewhere deep in his belly and the breath came hard against the ache in his chest. But there was still a little time. They were not yet in gun range and the hills were just ahead, scarcely two hundred yards. As he jumped for the saddle, and the girl got into hers, Teresa cried out again; Parras, distractedly whirling, saw far out to the left another laboring horse plunging toward them and remembered the man he had set afoot.

The girl and her father were already moving, banging the flanks of their mounts with spurred heels. Grabbing the dangle of reins with his left hand, Parras yanked the rifle sheathed under the fender and dropped onto a knee, settling himself to buy them some time.

He paid no attention to the man riding solo coming in from the left. Those others were nearer, already marked by the bright winks of muzzle flash as they tried against reason to drop the Romeros.

Frozen faced, Parras waited with the slugs whining around him. The three were fanning out now trying to make harder targets but Parras, lips bleakly twisted, continued holding his fire. If this move on their part was designed like their yells and wasted ammunition to rattle and panic him they were going to be in for some damned rude surprises.

Though touched with regret for the spot they had put him in, this repugnance was not going to alter his intention.

Killing, itself, it came over Parras weirdly, had never much bothered him. It was the thought, the grim concept, the projected necessity which most tried his patience: the idea of putting his hand to such butchery.

This was gnawing him now, trying to chew holes in the depths of his purpose, to sicken and scare him into giving it up — and only succeeding in turning him adamant.

Now he could see the pale blobs of their faces.

The one straight ahead, a wild burly shape in his leg-clutching trousers and steepled sombrero, was barreling straight on, zeroing in, plainly determined to run Parras down.

The fellow, teeth bared, was scarcely forty yards off when Parras squeezed down on the grip of his trigger, the recoil of that shot slamming hard through his shoulder.

The rider went off the rump of his mount with both arms outflung as Parras shifted the barrel to squeeze steel again, dropping the horse of the man's nearest flanker. The third gent whirled in almost comical alarm and was in the third jump of unconditional retreat when Parras knocked his horse sprawling. But the last one, the lone rider, was already gone when Parras' eyes searched for him.

Not until Parras had gone deep enough into the hills to be out of sight did Olivares — that wily fourth horseman — whip up enough ginger to emerge from the thicket into which he had fled when the gringo had stepped from his horse with that rifle.

Shaken and shuddering, stuffed with the outrage of mixed fright and fury, the mayordomo who'd aspired to become *hacendado* was still too confounded, too close to being dead, to marshal his thoughts into any coherence.

He had the look of a man just released from a nightmare, soaked in sweat, all his sap turned to jelly. He wouldn't have taken bets he hadn't dreamed the whole thing!

But he was sure enough he *hadn't* not to risk going nearer the two who had been unhorsed; that would put him, if Parras was waiting, directly in reach of that still warm gun.

CHAPTER
TWENTY-FIVE

But Parras wasn't waiting.

He had not even paused to consider the possibilities. Having no idea of that fourth horseman's identity Romero's gringo was following his nose through a trough between peaks with every bit of haste he dared risk. The girl bulked largest in the wheel of his thoughts — that old man, he was sure, would not be long in the saddle. At any moment he expected to find them, bogged down.

The flinty concussion of hoof on rock rang loud in his head as constant reminder of the men left behind and his own senseless softness; as the minutes began to pile up in his mind the sound pushed him into demanding more of his responsive mount than a horse on an uphill climb could afford.

Though he saw the folly in what he was doing, impatient concern would not let him desist. For he was sure, deep inside where these instincts were sharpest, that whatever he had given them back there would wear off.

He wasn't dealing with dudes. Those were hardcased men being paid for their toughness. They might come on with more caution but come on they would. He should have spilled all their horses.

He hadn't stopped to hunt tracks and now as the minutes stole toward the half hour and he was still without sight of the girl or her father he began to wonder if he'd come the right way. He fought off this worry for another quarter mile then pulled up and swung down. In the bright moonlight here the shale-strewn ground showed no sign of recent travel.

Parras, softly swearing, snapped a match to flame and crouching, anxiously peering, ran the cupped light back and forth, finding finally where a stone had been turned, continuing to search the baked ground until the match, burning out against fingers, was dropped.

Back in the saddle he stared long across his shoulder, studying the backtrail, ears stretched with listening. But the night had no news for him and, still undecided, he presently went on. He could not remember any place where they might have turned off, could not understand either how that misused old man could still be in the stirrups.

He wasn't.

Where the trail leveled off to shuck through the next hollow Parras saw them: dark shapes of two horses standing motionless without riders perhaps half a mile ahead. He put spurred heels to his mount.

He found the girl, softly crying, bent over Don Adolfo, and got down to look for himself. There was nothing he could do. The old man was past all earthly aid.

Parras, closing his mouth, settled into his boot heels, wanting to give her all the time he could. But without they moved along reasonably soon he could see how they might wind up like Romero . . . too dead to skin.

Gunplay was certain if those three he had spared should manage to get in sight of them again. No Christian sentiment would stand in their way and this time the boot might be on the other leg; you couldn't win them all no matter how good or lucky.

He cleared his throat but she paid no attention. He let another couple of minutes slip by. When she still crouched there with her papa's head in her lap he reluctantly touched her shoulder. "We're going to have to get going," he reminded her gruffly. "Some things don't wait around for nobody, and if those varmints back yonder are workin' for Olivares they won't be hankerin' to see you and me get clear."

She scrubbed at her eyes with the back of a hand and presently stood up to stare off across the hills. "Ground's pretty hard," Parras said, "but I'll — "

"We're not leaving him *here*," she said sharply, wheeling around to fix a black look on him. "He'll be buried with his father with a priest to — "

"We're not going to Two-Pole — "

"Papa is," she threw back at him flatly.

Parras looked like he thought she was crazy. "How's he fixin' to get there?"

"If you won't help I'll take him myself!"

Parras glared. Teresa said bitterly, "If you hadn't tied him head-down across that horse . . . "

160

There was thanks for you! "You claimin' I killed him?"

He looked thoroughly angry. Her woman's eyes weighed him. "Typical male reaction." She sniffed, and cocked her head to one side like she really was curious. "Why can't a man ever accept responsibility?"

"Why is some female always hangin' it 'round his neck!" Parras snapped, stomping off to fling into his saddle, snatching the reins up like a handful of snakes.

But he just couldn't go. Riled as he was he had to have a last look. By God, he might have known! There she was, making him feel like the world's lowest heel with her futile attempts to get the old man's limp cadaver off the hard ground.

Swearing under his breath, Parras got down, brushed her out of his path and picked up her father. But the rolling-eyed mount that had packed him before shied away with a snort when Parras moved toward him.

While he stood bitterly cursing, the girl caught the horse. She backed him up with her scarf folded over his vision, held his trembling weight steady while Parras retied the awkward burden securely. "Smartest thing we can do," he said gruffly, "is head for the countyseat and tell the whole story."

"We're taking him home."

No point in arguing with that tone of voice. Parras looked at her tiredly and finally, shrugging, got back on his horse. She would have the last word whether school kept or not.

He let her lead off with the old man in tow. But after a while sourly spent with glum thoughts, he pushed

161

forward to side her. "You got any notion where we're at?"

"Northwest of the ranch. Maybe three or four miles."

"When'd we cross the river?"

She whipped a look at him, startled. "I guess . . . I'd forgotten about that. We're northwest of it anyhow and — "

"Be light pretty quick. We'll be easier spotted. If that crew is still out beatin' the bushes we could be in real trouble . . . Some of that bunch wouldn't mind no more about shootin' a woman than they would about knockin' a steer in the head. And if they're back at the ranch, and we ride in, you'll be right where you started."

She dug up a wan smile. "What you're trying to say is — "

"I can say it," Parras grumbled. "You go into that place you're not comin' out, horseback or otherwise, without you sign the spread over or get a *señora* tacked onto your name."

Her eyes touched him slanchways. She said with confidence, "He wouldn't try that with you standing back of me."

"Who you think's been throwin' them slugs — bunch of prairie dogs, maybe? I might not be there very damn long! In the quick, anyway," he tacked on darkly. "He's in too deep to mealymouth now. We ought to go talk to the sheriff."

"Another gringo!"

"You're puttin' your chips on a gringo right now."

162

She bit her lip. "What makes you think you'd be able to convince him?"

"I could anyways try."

"Trying won't put much of a bulge in his pocket. He'll get no votes, Parras, listening to you."

"All right," he said. "You're calling the shots. If we got to play this your way the quicker we get back there the sooner it'll be over."

CHAPTER
TWENTY-SIX

The sun got up and dissipated the darkness with the brush of its smile, unfurling a blanket of workaday heat down across the gray miles of cracks and crevices, burning away the last droplets of moisture.

Parras' open-eyed stare took in roundabout cliffs, the gangrenous ochers relieved here and there by the blotched greens of juniper; the desolate emptiness that stretched out ahead was inescapably the road to his future.

He could look at this calmly with the sardonic humor of the man who had nothing and believed all trails led eventually to a grave. Where that might ultimately be made little difference to the fatalistic streak he was discovering in himself.

Which is not to say he was without apprehensions. He had the built-in fears common to most, but these were things he had learned to live with; that discipline showed in the clamped-tight fold of the broad-lipped mouth, but an uncaring will was brashly evident in the challenging way his look quartered these slopes. As they came out of the cut his stare hungrily embraced the dusty huddle of buildings that marked the headquarters of Two-Pole Pumpkin.

164

The place looked deserted and likely was if that bully-puss crew was still scouring the country, but Parras put little trust in appearances. He continued to search as they jogged slowly forward for the pale wink of metal, the flutter of motion that might signal waiting men.

He found nothing. Yet this hard show of vigilance was not relaxed. His look continued to pick and pry. This was the price a man paid for survival and he still nursed the memory of that fall from Tenkiller on a bullet-dropped horse. And that second narrow miss at the Roman Four cow hunt.

They rode into the yard and still nothing happened. With his stare again raking the somnolent look of these buldings, "Seems," he murmured, "like there's nobody home."

"Someone's been here," Teresa said jumpily. The edge in her voice brought his head around sharply.

"You sure?"

"You know the ground kind of gives where it's soft? I came over a place like that in the lane."

Parras turned his mount with the nudge of a knee and when he came back said, "Ground's been dug up and put back. Pretty recent. It's not the same color."

"I know."

They exchanged searching looks.

"You wait here," he said grimly, and rode toward the porch. It was like he remembered it. Like everything else. He swung watchfully down, hitched the horse on dropped reins, staring a while at the stable compound, the whitewashed adobe this spread used for a bunkhouse, the smithy and cook shack. He stood a final moment in an attitude of listening. Locusts in the cottonwoods, the thin whisper of trembling leaves.

Pretty well convinced they had the place to themselves, still with half his mind questing for answers, he crossed the warped boards and fisting his pistol shoved open the hall door. Finding no challenge he moved to the patio, again stopping to listen. He started opening rooms.

Three facts emerged from this activity: the office door was starred by a splintery bullet hole; a gob of dried blood stained the sill beneath the door to old man's bedroom; and there was no one, alive or dead, in the house.

He went outside and stared again toward the stables, irritably considering also the bunkhouse. He waved and, while Teresa crossed the yard, examined once more the tangled skein of bleak thoughts irrevocably tying him to the whims of this woman.

For she *was* a woman. Somewhere in those interminable hours of last night she had left all pretensions to girlhood behind. He watched the heavy breasts stir to the lift and fall of her breathing. "Someone," he said when she got off her horse, "holed up in the office. Door wasn't forced but there's been some blood spilled." He left it at that and half wheeled away to say over a shoulder, "You want . . . you want I should take care of him?"

"Do you think you could bring him into the house?"

Parras stood for a moment where the words had caught up with him. Without answering he went on,

166

hearing the skreak of the patio gate as he lifted the old man off the horse.

He could understand the need that was in her, deference to dignity, the compulsion to accord her father as many of the forms as circumstances permitted. You couldn't hold a man over in this weather very long. With no priest available she didn't want him put away like a piece of waste-paper.

Parras carried the dead man in through the patio and, following Teresa, laid him gently on the bed. Uneasy, bone weary, he left them there and retraced his steps, shutting the patio gate behind him. He could have done with some grub but, not wanting to remind her, took the horses across the yard in the direction of the stables, pausing when he got that far to assure himself there was no one lurking behind the closed door and windows of the bunkhouse.

If the horses had had any run left in them he probably would have left them where they'd been beside the porch, but they were too used up to count on. Pushed, they couldn't have gone half a mile. He left them standing on spraddled legs while he scouted the smithy and cook shack, finding both empty.

Coming out of the smithy he peered for long moments at the huddle of huts used to quarter the servants. The need in him for answers finally sent him toward these, but every one of them was empty as the hulls of shelled peas. Eyeing the pitiful belongings so obviously abandoned he reckoned these peons must have been considerably alarmed to have picked up and gone in such haste.

Eyes scrinching in brooding thought he walked moodily back, gathered up the horses' reins and took them to the stables. Something had happened around this place and whatever it was it must have been plenty bad.

He got the gear off the animals and put them in stalls. They would have been just as well left in the corrals where they could have rolled, but he thought it better not to advertise their presence. He found a brush and rubbed them down and when they had cooled enough took them out to the trough and let them drink. He forked hay for them back in the stalls and had just finished with this when the girl came in to say she had food on the table.

He followed her over to the house and back to the kitchen with its huge fireplace and the shiny black and nickel of a Yankee stove. Even the open windows did not seem very much to rid it of trapped heat.

He was in no mood to complain. He sat down with her and dug into the refried beans she had laced with salt pork and ate without talk until his plate was scraped clean It was a working man's meal and he did it full justice, afterward pushing back to roll up a smoke.

Her eyes looked a little red in this light. She only picked at her food. Parras presently said after a second cup of java, "What are your plans?"

Staring into her plate she shrugged without answering.

"You can't stay here."

She looked at him then. All the mixed up thoughts in her head looked at him. "I will."

Flat as the desert miles was that voice but he said to her irritably, "You told me once you were a prisoner here! You want to go back to that, or worse?"

"It's my home. I belong here."

Her mind seemed a thousand miles away.

"Can't you see you'll be playing right into their hands? Listen to me, Teresa. Olivares — "

"No one's keeping you here." With a little more life in her tone she said, "Go if you want."

He glared, then got up and tramped out of the house, half minded to. He said, "Damn it to hell, it's not my responsibility!" But he sat himself down on the edge of a step, knowing he was chained to this place just as she was, tied with invisible bonds like Teresa, held by the things they had been through together. No man who had any right to the name could ride off and leave her in this kind of fix.

"Women!" he said, and swore under his breath.

But he could see her side, too. The pride deep inside, the pride of the Romeros that would not let her give up this place to that treacherous cow boss without doing all that she could to . . . But what *could* she do? Put a bullet through him, maybe?

"By God!" Parras grunted. She was distraught enough to try it!

He got up, filled with futility, crossed to the stables and came out with a rifle. Not that it was like to do them much good. He might knock off a few but was much too practical to imagine he could stand off the whole hard-cased crew Olivares had assembled to make this deal stick.

He shook his head, still worrying about the departure of those peons. He didn't like at all the way this thing was shaping up. Nor — short of cutting his string — could he see any way of juggling the odds. He ought to put that girl on a horse and get out of here — but out *where?* and *what* horse? Those nags right now wouldn't take them a mile!

He took a look at the bullet scrape across his chest. It was weeping again where it had stuck to his shirt but he buttoned the cloth back over it. If he got out of this with nothing worse than that he'd be damned lucky!

This was as close to being hopeless as anything he'd known. He thought of hunting the shovel and having a dig out there in the lane but couldn't see how that would help. It was probably related either to that hole in the office door or the blood he had seen just outside the room where he'd left Don Adolfo.

He tried to think when he had slept last, and shook his head again. He was like those horses, dead on his feet. The only thing that kept him going was the picture of that girl trying to buck this deal without him.

CHAPTER
TWENTY-SEVEN

Somehow the day managed to drag itself past.

Parras spent most of it sitting on the porch with the rifle across his knees and, despite his good intentions, made a damn poor watchdog, continually dozing because he couldn't stay awake.

Each time he caught himself nodding he'd get up and, badly rattled, go and douse his head in the horse trough; this would help for a while, then he'd have it to do over. When Teresa called him in to supper he felt like a man coming out of a bender.

They ate without talk, neither one of them in the mood for it. The girl, it looked like, had been crying some more. Parras worried all the time they were eating. It just plain wasn't natural for the crew to be so long away. He couldn't keep from wondering if this extended absence didn't someway stem from that stretch of soft dirt out there in the lane.

Who the hell had been killed?

A part of his mind kept nagging him to look. Another part scoffed, deriding the idea that it could make any difference; hadn't he taken enough punishment already? He'd have plenty of shovel work planting Romero.

"Have you had any sleep?" he growled at Teresa.

Fatigue looked out of the pinched shape of her cheeks. She shrugged in lieu of reply and Parras said, "Better get some," dragging his spurs across the floor to the stove, frowningly pouring a fourth cup of Arbuckle, which he sloshed inside of him black and scalding.

From the stove he said in a tone of constraint, "When are you . . . uh, figurin' to . . . " and, not liking the projected sound of that, blurted, "Maybe I better go dig up a shovel."

When she didn't say anything he put the cup down on a corner of the table and went out feeling mean enough to kick Olivares clean to Frisco.

He found a pick and a shovel leaning against some sacked oats in a corner of the stable by the stationary ladder giving access to the loft. He saw the earth sticking to them and was reminded of the lane. He took a look at the horses and fed them some oats, giving each of them an armful of hay afterward. Then, carrying the tools, went to look for the graveyard.

It took him two hours to dig a satisfactory hole. When he finally stepped out of it he was sure enough bushed. With full dark not more than a quarter hour away he threw down the shovel and, peering at blistered palms, set out for the stables aching in every muscle.

He put halters on the horses and led them to the trough and, after they'd drank their fill, took them back and closed the doors. He picked up the rifle, thinking what a fool he'd been to go off without it. Carelessness of that kind was what got people killed.

172

He went back to the trough and splashed his face with water. Stood a while then looking and listening. Scowling and reluctant, he headed for the house.

No lights showing; she'd been smart about that. He wished she was smart enough to get the hell out of here — to make the attempt anyway, he thought dourly, and stepped onto the warped planking. He tried a match against the gloom, pushed open the door and made aching leg muscles take him to the patio.

A dim and sort of wavery glow outlined the open doorway of the room he'd put her father in. He moved toward this, anxious to get the man under ground. Maybe then she'd be ready to bend an ear to reason.

He jolted to a stop, one foot barely over the threshold, snatching back the curse that almost got away from him. The smoky, flickering yellow light of the solitary candle burning on a table at the foot of the bed gave the scene an eerie quality. Like a tableau glimpsed at a wax museum.

The old man was laid out in his best bib and tucker, ravaged face carefully washed, the hair brushed artfully back from his forehead, dead eyes closed like a man in sleep.

This was the way she wanted to remember him. But nothing, Parras knew, was going to erase the ugliness of the pictures still in her head. What she had done and was prepared to do now was not, he felt sure, an aspect of filial devotion; it was, rather, evidence of penitence for things she had thought and in rebellion probably said in the months she had yearned to get away from this place.

In this whispery light her hair looked black as an Indian's. She was standing, expressionless, back against the wall, staring into some hidden tunnel of necessity or despair, a crucifix clasped in white-knuckled hands. Perhaps she was silently saying Hail Mary's like they did with the beads, Parras thought, dragging his hat off, half turning then to set the rifle outside.

Resentment, apparent in the color of his neck, put him through the open door. Any feeling of guilt she was trying to get shed of was strictly her business. But staying here this long was about as crazy as a man ought to get, and if she figured to have him stay on riding herd while she held a private wake she better get straightened out!

"You through?" he growled, but had to ask her again before her sleepwalker's face came round to let that blank stare survey him. She stayed against the wall making no effort to comprehend or answer.

"Let's get this over." Parras moved toward the bed.

She spoke then, flatly, the words coming out through clenched teeth: "Leave him alone."

"Sometimes," he said, "You don't make much sense."

"No one expects you to understand, gringo."

"How long you aimin' to stand there?"

"That's for me to decide." She pulled up her chin. "I'll call when — "

"Then you better call quick. If you reckon to be up with him the rest of the night you can count me out!" he said, just as arrogant, and reached behind him to pick up the rifle.

With his hand scrabbling over the whitewashed adobes a sudden look of strain began to chew at his cheeks. His whole frame stiffened in that lopsided stance when a cat-and-mouse voice heavily freighted with satisfaction amusedly said, "It's not there, *amigo*."

An avalanche of preposterous notions whirled through Parras' aching skull while he stood locked in his tracks by those saturnine words. Chagrin, rebellion — a flood of conflicting urges pushed and pummeled at the gates of his caution; but to move was to die and only a fool would dare to think different.

"That's right," Olivares mocked, "be careful. Now! With the left hand, gringo, unbuckle that belt."

If Parras could have figured on even a halfway chance he might have tried to turn the tables, but the click of a six-shooter's drawn-back hammer warned him louder than words.

Shell belt and holster thumped the floor.

"Step out of it, man." The hated voice grinned.

Parras, filled with the churn of his wrath, complied.

"Get over beside Teresa and shove your chin against the wall."

Almost choking on spleen Parras once more obeyed and stood there crammed with futile fury.

"All right, Fay. Pick up his pistol." An obscene chuckle welled out of Olivares. "One wrong move is the limit in this game. Bet your chip, gingo, any time you feel lucky."

The thump and ching of spurred heels moved into the room, paused for brief seconds while leather skreaked, then carried a man's weight off behind the bed.

Chin to the wall, Parras stayed in his tracks.

"You can turn around now, mister," Olivares said.

"I'm surprised" — Parras sneered — "you ain't shot me already."

The mayordomo grinned. "I've a use for you, gringo."

"You can forget it right now."

"You'll cooperate, man, or go to Socorro charged with murder. And the girl will go with you charged as your accomplice."

Parras knew in his bones this fellow wasn't talking just to hear his head rattle. "What's the deal?" he said grimly.

"You're goin' to kill Madigan."

CHAPTER
TWENTY-EIGHT

There were a number of things Parras might have said but they all boiled down to the single word: "Why?"

"Because" — Olivares smiled thinly — "to keep this ranch solvent and find cash for my payroll Romero had to borrow from the bank on his cattle. A lot of these cattle have been run off by Madigan's Texicans to buy up the notes the bank held against your friend on the bed."

It was one thing to have suspected as much and quite another to have confirmation of this chicanery boldly delivered and hung around Madigan's neck by the fellow. Romero against this slippery pair hadn't the chance of a snowball in hell.

Parras' glance left the bed to brush across Joel Fay and the hungry look of the gun in his hand. How many of them were there? Why hadn't he heard horse sounds? Had they slipped in afoot, just these two, to glom onto him?

"If," Parras growled, "you can prove they've been rustling — "

"At this point I don't have to prove anything. I want those notes. You'll get them for me. Off his dead carcass."

"What makes you so sure?"

"I have the key piece." He grinned at Teresa and the twist of frightened hands clutched the crucifix more whitely. Olivares chuckled. "I don't much care whether you help me or not. I'll still have the girl."

"If you've got all the aces tucked away up your sleeve why are you botherin' to bargain with me?" Parras skeptically asked.

"A bargain," Olivares said, "usually implies some kind of give and take. I'm not giving you anything. It's been known for months the old Don's daughter would give the shirt off her back to get away from this place — you're not the first damn fool she's tempted. Twice men have been caught trying to make off with her. One got out of jail only last week. His signed statement is available if I should find myself hauled up before a court."

His eyes gleamed with triumph. "When a down-at-heels drifter got himself put on the payroll over my protests I was naturally suspicious. I had the man watched but in spite of my precautions he hatched up a plan with the girl's connivance to make it seem that her father — whom they'd secretly been plying with tequila — had wandered off into the desert, too drunk to know what he was doing.

"I was afraid for that man. I turned out the whole crew. For two days we searched, combing the chaparral. But a wind had been blowing. There were no tracks to get a lead from."

Olivares showed a crafty grin. "This, you understand, is the story I'll tell if I find myself in need of one. By the

178

time of the second night I'd become reasonably certain Romero was not in the desert. I began to wonder if indeed he had ever been. I may as well say I was badly worried. Keeping four of the crew I sent the rest into the hills. It seemed to me now the *patrón* had not left the ranch of his own intention.

"Though I was not at this juncture considering foul play" — Olivares had the temerity to chuckle — "I was about convinced he'd been the victim of a plot. I suspected this gringo, Parras, of removing the old man forcibly from his home.

"But where could they be hiding him? Don Adolfo had been in frail health for some time. Any long trip appeared extremely unlikely. Then I thought of Madigan.

"He was a Texican, too . . . like this gringo the girl had been seeing so much of. His crew was away, engaged in a cow hunt. All year we'd been feeling the inroads of rustlers; I knew my *segundo* thought Roman Four back of this. Was it too far afield, I asked myself, to imagine these Texicans — Parras and Madigan — to be in cahoots?

"I took my four men to Madigan's headquarters. There was nobody there — we searched every building. It was then I recalled an old haunt of *bandidos* we Romeros had cleaned out some years before.

"I set out at once with my four loyal *vaqueros*. At a point some miles from this abandoned hangout once again I divided my resources. Three men I dispatched to climb the bluffs above the creek, to head off this unnatural daughter and her lover, if my guess proved correct and the pair broke from cover. With my remaining *vaquero* — "

"I don't think," Parras growled, "I've ever met a gent so fond of his own voice. You mind if we sit down?"

Olivares grinned nastily. "We're just about to reach the meat of this business. To continue: with my remaining companion I tackled the approach in a more direct fashion, riding our horses down the bed of the stream. This had several advantages, but despite all our care the quarry was warned.

"As we came out of the creek, the ruined buildings to the left of us, the girl and her gringo — the old man roped to a led third horse — were already in flight, halfway to the bluffs. Parras opened fire and dropped my companion. The girl, with Romero, gained the slope, was lost to sight in the brush when Parras again fired, knocking the horse out from under me — "

"I'll bet you uncorked some real fancy lingo."

Olivares, darkening, went on. "With all of this racket it took me some while to catch the spooked mount of my companion. By the time I reached the top of the bluffs Parras and the girl had disappeared. Presently alerted by the sound of gunfire I saw them streaking into the desert, my three *vacqueros* after them. I put spurs to my horse. A cloud just then passed across the moon's face. When there was light again all six had vanished.

"I soon discovered they'd dropped into a wash. My horse was exhausted. I knew where that wash came out of the desert near a low ridge of hills not too far from Two-Pole Pumpkin. I took a short cut and came into

180

view just as my *vaqueros* broke out of the wash. As the girl, with her father still roped to his horse, went out of sight in the hills this gringo, Parras, flung off his mount and again opened fire. Luis, almost up to him, was knocked off his horse. The one just behind went down wildly screaming. The other *vaquero* was trying to get out of it when he was put afoot too.

"I was furious. But what could I do? Against a fellow as careless of killing as this gringo it was plain I hadn't a Chinaman's chance. With considerable reluctance I spurred off out of range. But as soon as Parras followed the girl into the hills I hastened back to my men.

"Luis was dead. We stopped long enough to bury him. While we were doing this, and patching up Felix, who'd been shot in the arm, my *segundo* Fay rode up with Luis' horse. He had been with the rest of the crew in those hills trying to find the *patrón*. He had heard the guns, then had found the horse and tracked him back to us. With both of us riding double, held to a walk by the condition of our mounts, we headed for the ranch to secure fresh horses, never dreaming we would find the people we'd been chasing sitting comfortably at home.

"But such was the case." Once more Olivares showed his thin smile. "It seems incredible. I could only assume they'd come back for fresh horses. But fate had stepped in. The old man was dead — of a stroke, I suppose. The girl and her Texican had apparently decided to brazen it out, probably hoping that in the poor light and excitement they had not been recognized.

181

"They had the old man in bed all washed and laid out, were holding a wake when we walked in on them. And do you know what they said? They insisted they had found Don Adolfo in the desert, dead from exposure! The desert Romero's crew had already searched!"

Parras, shaking his head, finally said, "Are you finished?"

"What more could I say? I've told the facts as we found them. The crew and the evidence will bear me out."

"You mean the dead horses?"

Olivares twisted a narrowed stare at him. "And the stiffs — the pair you killed right in front of my eyes. One is still where you dropped him. We can dig up the other if — "

"What about the pair you staked out with Romero?"

Olivares rubbed the side of his nose. "If you figure to tie Paco and Ramón to that deal you're going to look worse than you do right now. For your information I paid off those boys the day you rode over to join Madigan's cow hunt. Three of the crew wanted to stretch their damn necks. Fay claims they been working with the Roman Four bunch that's been lifting our cattle. I sent them packing. As the whole crew will testify. Told them to keep going if they valued their health."

"You been really sittin' up to this, ain't you? Feller slick as you is bound to have the answer to what happens to Madigan. I can't see you handin' me a

182

loaded pistol. What am I supposed to kill him with — my hands?"

"You'll find a way if you want Teresa here to keep breathing."

"What if I run out? What if the girl refuses to marry you?"

"I can take care of that, too. She won't be talking when the law shows up. Filled with guilt and remorse sitting here with her father, she turned against you. To shut her mouth you had to kill her. So run if you want to, gringo." He grinned.

CHAPTER
TWENTY-NINE

Although he'd said straightout he wasn't giving Parras a thing, in any course of action there always lies a choice. It may resemble jumping from the frying pan into the fire but, however improbable, the choice is there. Parras electing to go along with the man, said, "Where would I run to?" Joel Fay snickered.

Beneath his bristle of moustache Olivares' lips curled. "Don't burden me with your problems. All I want from you is those notes. And I'll be sending Fay with you to make sure I get them."

That this was news to the gunman was amply apparent. His unwelcome surprise fetched a short gruff laugh from Olivares. "It has always," he intoned, "been my earnest endeavor to leave as little as possible to chance. Should you fail in this, Parras, or attempt to cross me up, I know I can count on my friend Joel here to remedy the situation. As he'd be bound to do anyway if you elected to run."

This appeared to be less of a threat than a promise and directed, Parras reckoned, as much toward Fay as toward himself. Fay was being put on notice.

The mayordomo, blandly smiling, half turned to wave them through the door. Quick as a flash the girl flung her crucifix straight at his head. But Olivares, warned by the bulge of the gunfighter's stare, ducked under the missile and, wheeling with a snarled cry of "Bitch!" slapped her half across the room.

Parras, caught flat-footed by this explosive action, felt the gun in Fay's hand dig into his belly. *Getting old*, he thought, standing stiff in his tracks. The chance was lost; there wasn't a thing he could do about it now. Not with that gun snout dimpling his middle.

"Move out," Fay growled and Parras, seething, stumbled to the patio, helped by a shove. "Through the gate," Fay ordered, "an' head for the stables."

He was too old a hand and a heap too cagey to crowd Parras' heels close enough to be jumped. He'd welcome any excuse to put weight on that trigger — no one could want a job chancy as his.

Parras reckoned it was a time for discretion. Somewhere in the miles stretched between them and Madigan there might be a chance. It seemed highly unlikely there would be more than one. So it had better be good whatever he tried.

Crossing the yard, Parras glimpsed two spraddle-legged mounts with heads down by the porch and a shape with a rifle in the starlight behind. At least Olivares hadn't lied about that. So there had to be another hidden someplace in these shadows.

At the stables' open doors Fay said shortly, "There's a lantern on the doorpost. Put a match to it."

When the lantern was lighted and the wick adjusted Fay, still keeping his distance, said, "Put the gear on a pair of them horses," and stood off to one side while

Parras was busied with this. When all was in readiness, "Stand back," Fay ordered, and proceeded to test the girths for himself. "All right, climb aboard."

Outside, Parras asked: "Where are you pointing me?"

"Just foller your nose an' you'll get there."

They traversed the lane in single file, Indian style and just about as chummy. After a couple dozen minutes of riding without talk through the ghostly whispers of this starlit night Parras said, "This might not be too goddam smart. Has it occurred to you, Fay, we might be biting off more than we can chew? I mean," he grumbled when the man didn't answer, "if Madigan's found out the old Don is dead don't you reckon he just might be *expectin'* to get a visit?"

Fay refused to comment but presently brought his horse alongside, being careful to keep enough space between them to discourage any tricks a desperate man might think to launch.

But Fay was plainly nervous and this fidgeting uneasiness did not seem to be inspired by the company he kept so much as by things he kept looking for in the roundabout dark.

After half an hour of this nerve joggling progress Parras was fed up. "If you're expecting to be set upon I'm not goin' to be much help with an empty pistol."

Fay twisted a scowling look in his direction but continued to jog along without reply. He was riding now with a rifle across his crotch, its muzzle pointed naturally enough toward the gringo he'd been elected to keep in line.

186

Even through the endless churn of futile notions Parras found it somewhat weird to be riding with a man who looked like the most likely source of the blue whistlers fired during Parras' stint with the Roman Four roundup. Had the man been trying to kill him or trying only to scare him off? And whose idea was it? His own or Olivares'?

"You know," Parras said, "before we got back to Two-Pole Pumpkin someone else had been there. Must've been somethin' pretty wild goin' on by the looks of that blood."

Jolted out of himself Fay snapped: "What blood?"

"You didn't see it? Under the door to the old man's room. It's my notion someone got killed there. And there's a place in the lane where the ground's been dug up."

There wasn't much doubt about Fay's agitation. Why should this bother him unless he'd been present? "You want to tell me about it?" Parras chucked at him.

Fay's jaw snapped shut with an audible clack.

"We're in this together," Parras said persuasively. "If we pool what we know we might find a way out of this."

It was a forlorn kind of hope and Parras was not surprised when Fay refused the bait. Parras kept turning over thoughts for some way to reach him. Fay was a gun to be had for the hiring. Most of his kind would sell out if approached right, and he was under a forked stick, if the signs weren't lying.

Before Parras found an opening for pursuing this further both horses, twisting, threw up their heads,

187

nickering. Following the point of those whipped-forward ears he caught one confused glimpse of wheeling motion before the night tore apart in a racket of gunshots.

Twigs were clipped from brush at both sides of him, one slug slamming through the crown of his hat. He flung up a hand to keep from losing it just as Fay, swearing, barreled off through snapping branches. About to follow, some obscure thought sent Parras driving instead straight into the wink of those continuing explosions. "Here they are, boys!" he yelled. "Hurry it up an' we'll bag the whole lot of 'em!"

It was crazy, of course, the worst kind of folly, yet the incredible brashness of Parras' wild charge bred conviction; while off to the left Fay, in his flight, was making enough noise for at least half a regiment.

The dark shapes up ahead caromed off each other in a mangle of confusion to go tearing off in half a dozen directions, as madly spurring in their efforts to escape as though the Devil himself were breathing down their necks.

Parras pulled up and sat his panting horse with eyes shut, trying to control the stupid shudders that were shaking him. He felt weaker than a kitten in his near exhausted state, thinking how near he had come to being cut into dollrags. When he got enough wind back inside him to breathe with, instead of using this chance he had made for himself to get away from Joel Fay, he reined his horse after Olivares' pistolman, frequently pausing in this trek through the brush to call the fellow's name.

After some minutes spent in this fashion it did not appear likely that Fay was in earshot. But where the brush fell away to leave him stopped in the open Parras called once more, willing to risk whatever this shouting pulled out of the night if it might bring him to grips with some usable answers.

He could not have imagined that, ever loose of Fay's company, he would be so anxious to have the man back. But the gunman's reactions to that mention of blood and turned earth in the lane seemed to indicate knowledge Parras wanted to share if any way could be found of prising it out of him. The fellow might even be the very lever a man could use to free Teresa and Two-Pole Pumpkin . . .

The swish of a branch somewhere in the dark of the brush behind warned Parras he was no longer alone. Danger raced through the lock of taut muscles, but cogitation had sharpened his wits and he stayed as he was, wholly still in the saddle, saying tentatively, "Joel?"

"Get them paws up over your head!"

Fay's voice, all right. Crammed solid with distrust.

He came out of the shadows leading his horse, gun metal glinting from the hand at his hip. "You got rocks in your head? Yellin' my name out like that! I've got a good mind, by God — "

"You know who they were?"

" 'Course I know. Madigan's bunch."

"Then maybe we ought to try to get there ahead of them."

Fay's scowling stare showed the state of his nerves were nothing to fool with. "Of course," Parras said, "it's up to you. If you want to pull out . . . "

"I don't get this at all," the man growled, peering harder. "You had a chance to git loose; why the hell didn't you take it?"

"Maybe I've got a few bones to pick, too. You heard Olivares. He's got every bet coppered. Unless," Parras said to Fay softly, "you and me team up to throw a wrench in the works."

He was gambling Olivares had Fay over a barrel. Money wouldn't matter if Fay was in a bind; you could offer him a carload and never move him half an inch. He wasn't too bright, from what Parras had seen. The chance to get even, to get back some of his own on that master conniver, might appeal, Parras hoped, to the viciousness in him. He rasped a hand across one cheek. "If the two of us team up . . . "

He left it there, holding onto his breath.

Fay licked at cracked lips. "You mean grab them notes an' hang onto 'em? Thumb our noses at Polito?"

"It's a thought," Parras murmured. "Of course, there's more to it than that. He's dug in pretty strong with the crew to back him up."

"Not strong as he figures," Fay said with a curse. "I told him about the fight but he sure as hell don't know about MacGurdy!"

"MacGurdy? You lost me," Parras said, looking puzzled. "Where does *he* come into it? What fight was this?"

190

Fay scrinched up his eyes, still nervous and wary, patently tugged two ways by his urges. Caution and hate shone out of his stare. "How do I know this ain't some trick?"

"You figure I could trick a sharp feller like you?"

"You could damn well *try!*" Fay snarled, looking ugly.

"With my dukes gone to sleep? With nothin' in my belt but a empty shooter?" Parras let his lip curl. "Any nump could see the only chance we got of comin' out of this deal is to throw in together an' try to jerk the rug from under Olivares. 'Course, if you're silly enough to reckon you can ride out when he's through with you there ain't much point in me wastin' my breath."

Fay, chewing his cheek, stood a long time staring while Parras stared back in pretended indifference. "Don't do me no favors," grumbled Parras abruptly. "If you can't see the difference between a feller warped into the same boat with yourself and a jasper that aims to make coyote bait out of us, you deserve what you'll get."

CHAPTER
THIRTY

Gathering himself in a slither of muscles like a diamond-back coiling, Olivares' gunfighter glared in a frenzy of outrage. Not accustomed to having decisions forced upon him, the anguished process of making up his mind put a sheen of sweat across the drawn-back lips.

Torn between distrust and the hate that must have been prodding him for months, the violence inside him — inflamed by the gringo's tone and look — finally tipped the scales. He snarled, "I was inside the house! I didn't *see* what happened nor what brought it on — all I heard was the shootin'. It was Madigan's outfit!"

Parras lowered his arms with the breath running out of him. "If they found the crew gone, if they were figuring to take over, why didn't they stay?"

"How the hell would I know, bottled in that office? When them guns started poppin' I got outa there fast."

With Romero's notes in his pocket and no one around to contest his intentions — except maybe Fay holed up in the office — why would Madigan decide to haul freight? It just about had to be tied to that gunplay. "You don't think they were *driven* out maybe?"

192

"Besides Yorba there was eight men with Madigan. Who's goin' to push ten men armed outa that place?"

This was the snag that had been jabbing Parras. "Where was Madigan?"

"When the fireworks started him an' Yorba was inside — in the patio, I reckon, tryin' to figure how to git me outa that office."

"Maybe those two had a falling out . . . "

"Took more'n two guns to make that kinda racket."

"Was that banker still there?"

"Yeah. In his nightshirt. Out in the patio when I ducked for cover."

"Was he there when you left?"

"I didn't see him. Didn't look fer him. Alls I wanted right then was out!"

Parras scowled. That digging he'd engaged in should have been done in the lane after all, the way this looked to him now. "When you caught up to Olivares and told him about the shooting what did he say?"

"Just grunted, is all." Fay got back on his horse. "If we're goin' to grab Madigan we better git movin'."

"Reckon," Parras asked, "MacGurdy pulled out ahead of you, that he was gone when you left?"

"You think it was him they was shootin' at?"

"If it wasn't," Parras muttered, "I think we ought to talk with him. Don't suppose you'd consider going first to Socorro?"

"Them notes is what we better git first. Polito ain't the kind to let much grass grow under him. An' he don't believe in puttin' all his eggs in one basket. I wouldn't bet a nickel he ain't sent someone else."

Parras, thinking it over, was inclined to agree. He'd be wanting a double check on this; someone to do the job if they didn't. Someone to fetch the notes back to him and tidy up the scene to look like a shoot-out in the event he and Fay did what they were being sent over there for. And this was something he'd better remember if he hoped to walk away from this deal.

He looked up to discover the gunfighter eyeing him. With his pale stare puckered and tone reluctant Fay seemed to find himself forced to say, "Expect that now we're pardners you'll be wantin' some loads fer that pistol you're packin' . . . "

Considering the distrustful set of Fay's features the gringo shook his head.

"Reckon you'll feel a sight more comfortable if you keep those shells where they're at right now." He picked up his reins, squeezed his mount into motion.

Fay, staring after him, looked disconcerted. "You ain't figuring," he said, "are you, to go bracin' the likes of that son of a bitch with nothin' by Gawd but your two bare hands!"

"I figure to skin this cat without killin' him."

Fay, as they jogged along through the starlight, was being even more careful than Parras had counted on. Silent and watchful, he did not ride abreast but kept his horse half a length to the rear where any surprises Parras tried to cook up could be taken in stride and summarily dealt with.

This dog in the manger attitude wasn't going to make Parras' job any easier. He hadn't time to waste in regrets; and a man who made plans without knowing what he'd encounter was barking up a tree he'd likely not be able to climb. He'd have to see how the land lay and improvise from there.

He was up against two men, Madigan and Olivares, both of whom were trying to wind up with the Romero ranch; two men whose uneasy alliance in the theft of Romero cattle had long since ceased to be an advantage. It must have made Olivares furious to discover that Madigan's share of the loot was furnishing the wherewithal to buy up the old man's notes from the bank.

It was odd that Olivares, with so much sly cunning, had not thought of this himself. Perhaps he had. In any event it was obviously Madigan, if you could believe any part of this, who had wound up with the notes. And the notes were against cattle which the ranch could not produce. But this did not much improve Olivares' position. Unless he could prove the theft on Madigan . . .

Oho! Parras mused, beginning to see the light. He *could* prove it on him! Fay was the key. Fay was the go-between, the fellow who had fixed the steal up in the first place. Of course! And this must be what Olivares held over the man.

If Madigan, having moved at least a part of his crew into Romero's headquarters before inexplicably abandoning this advantage, expected to annex Two-Pole Pumpkin he would have to eliminate Olivares. Could this have been what all that shooting was about? Had

195

they fixed up a nasty surprise and moved out to give Olivares a chance to be caught in it?

Parras couldn't scare up any alternative explanation for Madigan's behavior that squared with known facts and made half as much sense. This wasn't a baited trap in the sense that a lure had been groomed to tempt the mayordomo. It hadn't been expected he'd discover they'd been around — or had it?

With his mind pawing over the things he had learned or had been told about this business, Parras had to concede the possibility. Once Fay's escape was known Madigan could expect Olivares' hired gun to make a beeline for his boss with the news of their visit and subsequent gunplay. At the time Madigan and that ax-faced Yorba had quit Two-Pole Pumpkin the man must have expected his outfit to ride Fay down.

None of this made a heap of difference to Parras. He had nearer things to worry about. Fay was the key to exposing the both of them; somehow he had to keep hold of the man and keep the little varmint alive if he could.

And he had to come up with some way to nab Madigan and get those notes off him. He racked his brain for some means of separating the man from his outfit, but got no place at all with that angle. Best he could settle for was the hope they might find him with the piece of a crew he had left at his cow camp: fellows like Deuce and those other hard workers who probably weren't in on the steal he had going.

Parras said over his shoulder, "Let's look in on that cow hunt. If we have to show up at his headquarters to nail him we might be bitin' off more'n we can chew."

He was agreeably surprised when Fay went along with this, having rather expected to have the suggestion chopped off at the pockets. Another quarter hour of unrelieved hoof sound and saddle skreak found him picking at it, fretful, increasingly dissatisfied, uneasily wondering what purpose of Fay's this could serve, to make him willing to let it stand.

CHAPTER
THIRTY-ONE

It seemed to Parras, peering through branches at the Roman Four wagon, that perhaps at last his luck might be on the upswing.

Half a mile out across the glimmery flat indistinct riders, hunched in saddlers, interminably circled the two bedded herds. Nearer, seen more clearly in the moon's brightening light, two men stood talking, tin cups in hand, by the wagon's tailgate. Parras directed a questioning look at the gunfighter.

Fay, breathing hard, took anoother squint and nodded. "It's Yorba and Madigan, all right."

Parras reckoned the riders would likely stay with the cattle. "What about Coosie?"

"Cook won't stir. He don't like that pair no better'n I do."

"All right," Parras murmured. "Let me do the talking when we get down there."

"Get yourself shot up if that's the way you want it. I'm stickin' right here. Whatever talkin' I do will be done with a rifle."

Parras stared, bitterly angry. He should have reckoned on something like this. A lot of wild thoughts slammed around in his head but only fools argued with a loaded gun.

"I don't think — "

"Think what you please. I wouldn't trust that pair any farther'n I could throw 'em."

Shrugging, Parras walked his horse into the open. He pushed the man out of his mind, giving all his attention to the shapes by the wagon, watching for the first indication of their intentions.

He was halfway across the hundred feet when the Roman Four ramrod, Yorba, glanced up and saw him, visibly stiffening. Alerted, Madigan twisted his head, right hand starting beltward. It stopped partway, spread and motionless, as Parras sang out: "It's Walt Parras. Got somethin' you better listen to."

By the time he got this much of it said he was quitting the saddle, ten feet away from them, close enough now to see the scowls on their faces.

He let go his mount's reins. "You act like you didn't figure to see me again."

"What the hell do you want?" Madigan said gruffly.

"I want those notes you bought off MacGurdy." He was counting on shock and saw it hit both of them. Madigan began to swell like a toad. Parras drawled, "Before you boys get off on the wrong foot you might like to know I'm not here by myself."

Madigan hauled a great breath deep into him, but it was Yorba who had to make good; Parras' cold-eyed attention never left him for an instant.

He watched color surge into that self-certain face and, standing there, trying to appear confidently indifferent with an empty pistol stuffed in his holster, saw a brightening shine maliciously burning in those cynical eyes as the man's rimless mouth loosed a spate of foul invective.

Madigan's move, when it came, almost took him unawares.

Moonlight skittering off a line of lifting metal apprised him of his peril and he wheeled with that glimpse, flinging himself aside just as flame lanced from the snout of it — but this took his eyes off Yorba.

Something exploded against the side of his head and he went to his knees, all his joints loosening in a kind of red fog. Through a darkening vision laced with bright flares the gun-weighted fist of the Roman Four ramrod chopped at him again. He tried to throw up an arm. Shouts banged against the walls of his skull. He tried to kick his way free and felt himself dropping through a cavernous dark . . .

He probably wasn't out much longer than it would take to jerk the head off a turkey. The moon didn't look to have moved at all, and when he clawed to an elbow to peer toward the cattle the men riding herd were standing in their stirrups, stopped and staring. Then, in tightening awareness, he saw the bent back of a half squatting man going through Kurt Madigan's pockets, scarcely three feet away.

The sight of that man drove through him like corn squeezings sloshing into an empty stomach, and all the weeks he'd spent tracking him through one cow camp after another came crowding in to shake every lesser need clean out of mind. In this sharpening focus all else

200

fell away in the bitter remembrance of how the trail had played out two years ago at Corpus.

Figuring the man either dead or in prison, he'd gone on to other things until that note from Farnol had taken him into Shakespeare six, seven weeks ago to learn from Idewall Jones that the fellow had been sighted a fortnight previous in Dos Cabezas. The price had jumped to ten thousand dollars but he was gone when Parras checked; no one he'd spoken to had ever heard of Jake Frezanno — or if they had they were not admitting it. Then he'd gotten that tip two weeks ago from Murnam and the trail had fetched him here.

To wind up with a dead horse at the foot of Tenkiller.

Parras stared at the rifle beside Fay's leg and knew in his bones he would never move quick enough. This was when he remembered Teresa cooped up at the ranch with that bastard Olivares. He would damn well be no good to her dead — nor would Fay with that stuff locked in his noggin!

A grunt came out of Fay, crammed with satisfaction, and the man — still squatting — reared back with his fists full of papers. There would never be a better chance than now, Parras knew, but when he reached for the pistol it was no longer in his holster.

If the gunfighter turned to find him teetering on bent knees there would be no time for talking. Man had what he wanted, what he'd gunned Madigan and Yorba down for. To leave another gut-shot corpse behind wouldn't bother this whippoorwill one goddam bit!

Parras, waiting no longer, launched himself in a desperate lunge. The crash of impact flung Fay forward, grinding his chin into shaley ground with Parras' left arm locked under his jaw, right hand clamped to Fay's straining wrist, striving frantically to keep the nearly drawn weapon from clearing its holster.

Unobserved, two of the circle-riders had given up looking and were on their way over. Even if Fay or Parras had noticed, it would not materially have changed anything; both were completely engaged, gasping, grunting, each striving with everything he had, desperate in the enormity of what could be lost.

Parras was bigger, heavier boned, essentially the stronger, but the lumps he had taken, the lack of adequate rest, had him dangerously close to being out on his feet. The gunfighter, shorter, lean as a hunting cat, had a wiry resilience that could bend like a whip; this — spurred by the prize he had just got off Madigan plus the fury unleashed by the gringo's attack — gave him every right to feel the eventual outcome would find him victor.

The only thing Parras had going for him now were the grips he had taken with his initial advantage and he was using up fast just trying to hang on.

Fay bucked and twisted like a sunfishing bronc. Trying to keep that lock on the man's neck and jaw, Parras couldn't bring enough weight or leverage to keep the gun where he'd had it. Fay's sweat-slippery wrist had the pistol's barrel entirely clear and was striving to free his hand.

Parras had to relinquish the grip on Fay's neck and the man, twisting under him, arched his back, heaving, dislodging the cramping bulk of his antagonist, trying

202

to swing himself into a roll that would free the wrist to let him bring up the gun.

But Parras locked his left fist around the barrel, thwarting the attempt although unable to wrest the weapon away from him. Fay banged his head into Parras' face, nearly sending Parras out of his skull with the pain. Then Fay began slugging and a red mist threatened to shut off Parras' sight. Yet he knew if he brought up either hand he was done for.

It began to seem like he was done for whether he brought one up or not.

He tried to fetch up a knee but Fay was too quick for him. Yet this very alacrity gave Parras his chance. Parras feinted another try for the groin; when Fay jerked back Parras went with him, smashing Fay's clenched fist, knuckles down, against a rock. The man yelled. The gun slipped from his grip as Fay's whole body recoiled. And the next thing Fay knew he was staring down its muzzle.

"Don't move — don't even blink!" Parras rasped, coming onto a knee.

CHAPTER
THIRTY-TWO

No hydrophobic skunk ever looked half as mean, Parras thought, as this kill-crazy gunfighter brought to full stop.

Pushing onto his feet with the air sawing in and out of his chest, Parras stood there a moment catching up with himself. Doubling the hazards, taking wild chances, looked like a pretty dubious kind of procedure, but what other way was there? Olivares had to be pulled off her back and, in view of the lies the man had armed himself with, this gun-handy dog had to be kept alive.

But no rules said Fay had to be told this.

"You can pick up those papers for a starter," Parras told him, never taking his glance from that venomous stare. "Just keep one thing in mind: you'll pack easier *dead*."

Fay, cheeks livid, finally shoved to his knees and, scrabbling about like a broken-backed crab, began retrieving what he'd taken from Madigan's pockets. Twice his hand passed Parras' dropped pistol but he presently got up without having touched it to hold out Romero's notes.

"You took 'em," Parras said; "you hold onto them."

The first inkling he had that someone was behind him came when Fay, staring past Parras' shoulder, cried: "You goin' to set there an' let this drygulcher git away with it?"

Starting to stiffen, Parras coldly grinned. "Nice try, Jake, but — " and he let the rest go when leather skreaked back of him. It woke something near to savagery in him and he rasped through thinned lips, "You can bet your bottom dollar if I get knocked over I'll be taking this son of a bitch right along with me!"

It was Deuce that answered. "Otherwise what you figurin't' do?"

A prickly itch got between Parras' shoulders. "He's got an overdue date with the hangman at Prescott."

"You a Federal marshal?" Deuce's partner, Nevada, asked.

Knowing this pair, having hunted cows with them, Parras was tempted. Accepting the label might just keep them out of this, but what he most needed right now was help. "Just a private citizen," he growled, drawing back the hammer, "but if I get any interference I'm lettin' this whip-poorwill have it."

"There's handier holes right here t' drop him into. We seen what he done — go ahead an' plug him." Nevada spoke cynically. "Why load yourself down with a skunk like that?"

Fay's gaze rolled around. He worked a cottony tongue across cracked lips with both bugged-out eyes dreadfully clinging to that held-back hammer under Parras' thumb. "Boys — " he gasped. "Turn me loose and you'll never have t' do another day's — "

"I'd rather work than be dead," scoffed Deuce from the saddle.

"Parras," Nevada called, "one'll get you five nobody at Prescott'll ever see this gook. Why don't we just bury the bastard right here?"

The man's horse came nearer, the projected shadow reaching out across moonlit ground to show a lifting rifle. With a guttural snarl Fay whirled in his tracks. Before he had gone five jumps in his fright a noose snagged one of his ankles, upending him.

Fay let out a rabbit squeak as Parras' bleak turn covered Deuce with the pistol. "Shake it off," he said, ignoring Nevada. "Olivares is holding the Romero girl hostage against this bastard's safe return."

For a couple of moments there was pregnant quiet. Someone sighed. Deuce gave a flip to his rope, reeled it in. "Stay right where you're at," Parras gruffed at the gun-fighter, and went on to pick up the dropped pistol and rifle. He shoved the six-shooter into his belt, shook the loads from Fay's weapons and flung the hardware back to its owner. "Pick them up and get into your saddle."

He took a look at the others. "Case you boys are looking for work there's fifteen bucks apiece in it for you if you want to come along and make sure he gets delivered."

The pair swapped glances. Nevada nodded. Deuce said, "What about Madigan an' Yorba?"

"They'll keep," Parras said. "That girl needs help."

The night was near spent but there were lights in the house when Parras' cavalcade came in sight of the

Romero headquarters. Pulled up, Parras dug out what was left of his funds and "Just in case" passed half to both of the Roman Four punchers.

"This could get a mite sticky if some of those ridge-runners Olivares hired happen to be staked out in those shadows. Fay and me better ride in alone. I'd like them to think he's still tall in the saddle. Give us five minutes to get in the house, then raise all the hell you figure you can handle."

"What happens t' me?" Fay wanted to know, his gunfighter's stare turned spooky again.

"Depends on you. Only promise I'm making is if you throw a wrench it'll be the last one you ever put fist to."

He rode into the open feeling like a fish in half a barrel of water. He put his mount up the lane, hearing Fay's horse making tracks just behind. He said in guarded voice from the corner of his mouth, "When we get down at the veranda act like you're boss for Chrissake or we're both dead."

He could feel the man's hate like cold wind curling around him and the man's jumpy nerves held little promise of leaving him much margin. Still walking his horse he turned into the yard. No sound leaked out of the roundabout shadows that hung like crouched men in this heart-thumping quiet. With the porch just ahead the snarl of Fay's voice rasped, "Be goddam careful how you quit that saddle."

Then the porch was in front of them and Parras still hadn't glimpsed any flutters of movement. But his mind hadn't changed much — not with this feel of unseen eyes digging into him.

He stepped out of the saddle, Fay dismounting behind him. Parras, chancing a glance, saw the gun in Fay's fist. This appeared natural enough but failed to reassure him. There was still the dark hall ahead to be gone through and who could guess what Fay might try in that stygian gloom?

He stepped onto the porch, the planks groaning under him.

The gunfighter back of him lifted a call. "Fay out here — with that gringo. We're comin' in." He prodded Parras' spine with the snout of his six-shooter; even knowing it was empty afforded Parras no consolation. "On your way, bucko. Straight down the hall — an' don't forgit I can see every thought you flip over."

Parras wished he could feel half as sure about Fay. He pushed open the door, every nerve twisted tight, and knew the man had the right of it. That patch of moonlit patio at the corridor's end was going to silhouette his shape and neatly set him up for whatever try Fay had in mind.

He'd been a fool not to think of this, and heard Fay chuckle. That the sound was jumpy with tension did not soothe Parras' own nerves much.

"Go on!" Fay snarled. "Git movin', damn you!"

There wasn't much else Parras *could* do short of throwing in his hand.

He stepped through the door with every muscle screaming protest, every inch of flesh aquiver, striding on stiff legs toward that moon-bright oblong marking the hall's far end.

208

And astonishedly reached it without Fay having tried a goddam thing!

He wheeled into the patio, the ching and dragged rasp of Fay's spurs right behind him, his mind worrying about Fay's failure to act while so much was so heavily stacked in his favor.

With those notes in his pocket and the gringo disposed of Fay could have suckered Olivares with any yarn he chose — at least he might have thought to. Fay's whole life, Parras suspected, had been bent to cut and run. The fellow demonstrably was a bushwacker, the kind who got in his best licks from ambush. Hadn't he just cut down Kurt Madigan and Yorba with no more compunction than you'd get from a rabid dog? And the threat represented by either or both wouldn't hold a patch to what Fay could look for if Parras came out on top in this tussle.

So why had he passed up the best chance he'd have?

It bothered Parras, confounding him, to discover the man so far off his bent. If he wound up at Prescott Fay'd be hanged and knew it. So why would he string along this way? Could a man believe it was *fear* cramped his style?

Parras couldn't. He had never met up with that sort of fright. He would rather imagine the man hadn't heard of him or failed to connect Parras up with his past. Even so, without he was simple as Simon, Fay had to know that in the dark of the hall he'd had the gringo right where he'd wanted him. One good rap with the barrel of that hogleg would have turned Fay loose to play any game he wanted.

"Over here," Fay ordered, waving his gun toward Romero's bedroom. Eyeing him, suddenly askance, Parras' mouth tightened up with the suspicion of something he should have thought about before.

To approach this place with any hope of helping Teresa it would have to seem to Olivares — and whoever else might see them — that Fay was still pushing Parras around. To make this illusion sufficiently convincing, Parras had tossed the man his own beltful of cartridges before they started up the lane, intending, of course, to keep a weather eye peeled.

It was still only guesswork, but if Fay had any wheels at all in his thinkbox he had used their trek through the dark of that passage to get at least one load under the hammer.

Parras guessed he should be shot for the simples. The part that really got its thumb in his eye was the indisputable knowledge that there was no way he could check on this without alerting Olivares. It worried him enough that he even considered ordering Fay to throw down the gun, which Fay wouldn't of course if it was any good to him; but ere Parras could embark on so desperate a measure the restless probe of his curving stare picked up the steeple-hatted sentry, Winchester in elbow crook, holding down the well rim, bowed legs dangling, the black pebbles of those eyes fixed unreadably upon him.

Parras recognized the man as one of the pair he had unhorsed and had little doubt the fellow would relish paying him back — given the flimsiest excuse. Olivares wasn't one for leaving much to chance.

Parras pushed open the door of Romero's room. Candles still burned at the foot of the bed. Nothing appeared to have greatly changed.

Don Adolfo still lay in state; the girl with her unblinking sleep-walker's eyes crouched, as before, against the far wall; and the mayordomo's potbellied shape, oozing satisfaction, considered the gringo with spurious good humor.

"Tell me, bounty hunter, did you take care of Madigan?"

Parras felt like groaning. Everything needed to blow this deal hell west and crooked was right here confronting him, ready to go off like a four-alarm fire. If Fay hadn't been so goddam stupid or so caught up in his greed for those notes . . .

Regrets weren't going to burst any six-guns. Unless Parras could avert the intended disaster this fat little Mexican had so artfully contrived, the girl, Frezanno and himself were due to head for glory on a cloud of stinking power-smoke.

But how to prevent this? Where to begin? Which prod to use first?

With that opening salvo Olivares had cut half the ground from under Parras, making impossible any sort of coup counting on help from that woman-killing bastard who called himself Fay. With the kind of money held out for his pelt Jake Frezanno wasn't about to throw in with one who made his living from rewards other men weren't bold enough to go after.

Parras didn't feel very bold right now. The single slim chance Olivares hadn't allowed for were the loads in the pistol in Parras' waistband. Yet with his mind such a hodgepodge of half-glimpsed truths and crackpot notions almost anything Parras tried could launch the very cataclysm he'd been trying so frantically to avoid.

Olivares, watching him, chuckled: the sound of a man who had carefully done his homework and could now await with confidence the planned and inevitable outcome.

Fay was intended to rid the world of this gringo, and Fay had a loaded gun in his fist.

Parras' eyes, red rimmed, had a hard time tracking; he had to make a conscious effort just to keep them open. Yet it was all too apparent he could not wait longer on the overdue distraction Deuce and Nevada had been primed to provide.

It was the thought of that loaded gun at his back that drove Parras into his sudden avalanche of words. "You know I wouldn't be here otherwise!" he cried. "It wasn't Romero's notes was bothering you — they could have been gotten without killing anyone. You had to have both of them damn well dead to be sure you weren't tied into that cow stealing!"

He hoped to hell that numbskull was getting this. With a grimace he twisted the barb a bit deeper. "Ought to give you a laugh to know Fay was the chump fool enough to kill both of 'em, never guessing he'd been pointed to go the same route!"

The quiet grew and grew and became so acute the only thing Parras could track was the thump and bump of his own pounding heart.

212

Caught like the gringo, empty-handed in the path of a plan gone off the rails of its predetermined course, Olivares hung there, moon faced, filled with his first wild look of uncertainty, rigid as some phantom in a wax museum. The confidence fell out of his face, his eyes began to bulge with fright.

A sound of hooves crunched through the night.

The girl, springing frantically away from the wall, sent the table crashing from the foot of the bed, followed the guttering tumble of candles to the floor as powder bursts hurled their explosions across the yard.

Parras dropped as Fay's gun kicked clamor through the outside sounds and beyond him somewhere a second gun spoke. Parras' shot, angling upward into the blackness behind that flash, thumped a gasp from Olivares.

"Parras!" Fay shouted; and through the cacophony of settling turmoil could be heard a rumble of bickering voices. As Parras caught at Fay's leg the man's gun angrily spat again.

Fay's terrified yank snatched the boot from his grasp. "Stop, you damn fool!" Parras yelled, a vision etched on his mind of the man perched on that well rim — but Fay was already half through the door charging straight into the eye of that rifle.

Time Parras found the lamp, got it lighted and bent to help the shivering girl to her feet Deuce and Nevada were pushing into the room behind the slat shape of a nervous, scowling badge-toter. "Deputy Scroggins," Nevada said. "This here's Walt Parras."

The deputy, glancing toward the bed, pulled his hat off. "Sorry about your father, ma'am." His hard look slid into an inspection of Parras. Touching the mayordomo's slack bulk with the toe of a boot he said: "You kill this feller?"

"Looks, anyway, like I'm stuck with it."

"I wouldn't work up no sweat. Taken quite a spell but we finally uncovered enough tracks to move in on him. Sheriff was here the other night with a warrant . . . sheriff an' a deputy that never come back. Know anything about 'em?"

"'Fraid not," Parras said. "Nothing I could prove anyway. Feller outside the door was here, barricaded in the office by his tell of it. Said it was Roman Four done that shooting. Said a lot of things though, besides his prayers."

"You're talking about the jigger that killed Madigan and Yorba?"

"That's right." Deuce or Nevada could have put him next to that.

"How much do you know about the old man's death?" Scroggins asked with a slanchways excursion of his eyes toward the bed.

Parras shrugged. "When Romero disappeared Olivares gave out he'd wandered off into the desert. Girl didn't believe it. She came after me at the Roman Four cow hunt."

It interested Parras the way the man's stare kept juning around the crumpled shape of the mayordomo without ever quite lifting all the way to his own. He couldn't see why the man should be afraid of him. He

214

said, "The two of us came up with Romero at that old rustler hangout on the Animas. He was in a bad way. Heart give out while we was fetching him home."

If the deputy thought it weird the way Teresa mechanically appeared to nod agreement whenever Parras paused he was polite enough to underline this with a question. Perhaps he subscribed to the unspoken notion that some sleeping dogs were better left alone.

"What you figurin' to do now?" he said to Parras.

"Still a lot of hills I ain't seen the other side of. First off, though, I'm going to have to get up to Prescott. If you've any reason for curtailin' my movements . . . ?"

"I think not," Scroggins said. "What's Miz Romero going to do for a crew?"

"I expect Deuce here and Nevada will likely stick around till things shake into some acceptable pattern."

"Yeah. Well, guess I better be headin' for the countyseat with my report," Scroggins said and went out, Deuce and Nevada tramping out after him.

Parras trailed them to the patio, standing around in a preoccupied fashion while sound of the posse moved off up the lane. The dreary gray look of another day was being replaced with a brighter glow along the dark scarps, and a wind up there reminded him winter would soon be tramping over this country.

Standing alone, still thinking about it, Parras wondered if it was the sheriff, his bushwhacked deputy or Sig MacGurdy, the Socorro banker, out there under that soft ground in the lane.

He saw the lamp go out in Romero's room. Teresa came to stand with her back against the doorpost; it turned him edgily restless the way those dark eyes enigmatically considered him. With more in her voice than he had ever heard there she asked, "What would you find somewhere else that isn't here?"

Time to be getting Fay roped across a saddle.

"I'll let you know," he said, "when I get there."

About the Author

Nelson Nye is an author of Westerns who has been himself a rancher, cattle-puncher, horse-breeder, and all-round son of the real West. He's an authority on quarter horses and used to raise them on his own ranch. Now he lives in Tuscon, Arizona, and does most of his riding on the keys of a typewriter. He's the book reviewer of the Tombstone *Epitaph*, and one of the guiding lights of the Western Writers of America.

Nelse has had quite a raft of good novels published under his own signature and a few pen-names as well, and is quite proud of having won the WWA Spur Award for one of them. He is the 1968 winner of the Golden Saddleman Award, which goes to the person who has contributed most to the field of Western Americana.